THE RIVER MEN

Twenty-seven robberies, fifteen cargo broaches, and seven cases of murder: not in the past fifty years has there been such an outbreak of thieving and crime on the Thames; and in no single instance has the culprit been brought to justice, or his identity discovered. A new criminal organization with a mystery man at its head is playing the London river police for fools — and the latest officer on the case has been murdered, his body weighted and sunk in the river. Such is the challenge facing Inspector Terry Ward . . .

GERALD VERNER

THE
RIVER MEN

Complete and Unabridged

LINFORD
Leicester

First published in Great Britain

First Linford Edition
published 2019

A catalogue record for this book is available
from the British Library.

ISBN 978–1–4448–4172–5

1

Gallows Wharf

The morning was cold and raw, with a thin mist that hung over the Thames partly obscuring the silent wharves and deserted warehouses that lined the banks of the river in Greenwich Reach, softening their ugly lines and lending to them a dignity that was lacking in the revealing light of day. Somewhere in the east the sun was rising, but as yet no hint of the coming dawn was visible in the dark sky. The river slept, though in less than an hour it would be waking to the clamour of another day of toil.

Already, further up towards the Pool, splashes of light marked the places where the big cargo boats had been loading and unloading for the greater part of the night. Here the squeak and rattle of derricks, the muffled voices of men shouting orders and the bumping and scraping of heavy cargo broke the stillness which further downstream in the Reach was only disturbed by the lapping water as it swirled round the rotting piles of the wharves and rippled against the blunt noses of the barges as they strained at their creaking moorings. Presently Billingsgate Market would splutter to life under the cold glare of many arcs, and along the mist-shrouded banks other lights would be springing up to remain twinkling blearily until the daylight came to rob them of their usefulness.

The first hint of grey was low in the sky when a dinghy came nosing stealthily through the thin fog, moving downstream in the direction of Deptford Creek. The solitary man at the oars was obviously an experienced waterman, for he rowed with long, even strokes, and the dip of his sculls were scarcely audible. He kept close in to the Surrey shore, passing under the shadow of the moored barges, his eyes peering through the murk at the nearby bank.

He was an unprepossessing individual. A ragged cap covered his matted hair; the grime of his skin blended with the stubble of beard that covered face and jaw. A thick blue jersey and a pair of dungaree trousers constituted his clothing, and the knitted fabric revealed the strength of his broad chest and brawny arms. His eyes were small and keen, and the expression of his face was forbidding.

Two hundred yards away from Greenwich Pier, he stopped the rhythmic motion of his oars and scanned the gloomy bank. It was obvious that he had found what he sought, for after a moment's pause he pulled in to the shore, skilfully manoeuvred the little boat among a forest of weed-covered piles that supported a crazy building jutting out over the water, and tied up to a rusty ring that was bolted through one of them. Shipping his sculls, he stood up in the swaying craft and looked about him. In the darkness, three feet above his head, he could sense rather than see the timber floor of the building which the piles supported — a gaunt, dilapidated warehouse, built in the eighties and known locally as Gallows Wharf.

The name was misleading, for no

gibbet had ever stood on the site of this ancient structure. It had originated from a corruption of the name of the man who had built it, a riverside merchant called Callers, who had used the place as a repository for grain. In those days, Gallows Wharf had been a hive of industry, and at most hours of the day and night had resounded to the noise of men labouring to unload or load the innumerable barges tied up at the long frontage. Even now, from an upper floor of the warehouse, the broken grain chute still projected like the decaying beak of some prehistoric bird.

Upon the death of its original owner, there had been a legal dispute regarding the property, and it had been thrown into Chancery, remaining empty, and so far as was publicly known un-tenanted, falling more and more into disrepair as the years went by. The activities that went on in the immediate neighbourhood were conspicuous by their absence at Gallows Wharf. The dirt-crusted windows, the majority of them glassless, looked out blindly over the oily water. No barges tied up at the broken frontage, and the big gates that opened into Thames Street were kept permanently locked. The building was a derelict, slowly rotting to destruction.

The man who in the early hours of this cold February morning had come to such an unprofitable place reached up a hand and groped among the slimy piles. His searching fingers presently found what he was seeking, a bell-push screwed into the oozy wood; an unexpected object in such a place, but it apparently afforded him no surprise. Three times he pressed the little button, two short presses and a long one, and waited, holding on to one of the piles to retain his balance.

There was a short interval, and then there came to his ears the soft thud of a footfall overhead. The rasp of a bolt followed, and a section of the wooden roof began to rise slowly.

'Who's that?' asked a harsh, thin voice.

'Limmer,' muttered the man in the boat. 'I've come from Copping.'

An oblong trap which had been open a few inches was swung back and a rope

5

ladder dropped, one end falling into the dinghy. The waterman climbed laboriously up the wooden rungs and hoisted himself with difficulty through the aperture into the room above.

It was a huge apartment, originally the main storeroom of the warehouse, now a draughty, cavernous place of many shadows that a single candle burning on a bare deal-topped table did little to dispel. A thick layer of dust covered the broken floor, and ancient sacks of mildewed, rotting grain were stacked round the walls.

The newcomer gave a quick, disparaging glance round the place and then watched in silence while the man who had admitted him pulled up the ladder and closed the trap. He was an old man with stooping shoulders and a lined yellow face. The feeble glimmer of the guttering candle glistened on his bald head and showed the fringe of grey hair that grew irregularly round the base of his skull. He was dressed in a rusty black overcoat that had seen much service, and his hands were covered by gloves of the same hue. Around his neck he wore a greasy muffler that was knotted closely under the protruding chin. Straightening up, he shuffled over to a chair behind the table, sat down, and surveyed his visitor keenly from under bushy eyebrows.

'Well?' He jerked the single word out sharply without taking his eyes from the other's face.

The waterman looked at the floor, avoiding the keen scrutiny, and shuffled his feet uneasily. 'I was told if I come along you'd be able to fix me,' he muttered after a pause.

'Fix you? What do you mean, fix you?' snapped the old man.

The man in the blue jersey raised his eyes. 'I've got some stuff. Off one of the Dutch boats. It ain't worth a fortune, but — '

'Who told you about me?' interrupted the man at the table. 'Copping?'

The other nodded.

'He told you to come to me, did he?' grunted the old man. 'What did you say your name was?'

'Limmer,' answered the visitor.

'Limmer. I've never heard of you before. You're not one of the regulars?'

'I 'ad a job until two months ago,' answered the waterman. 'Workin' on a collier.'

'How did you lose it?' The yellow face was thrust forward as the question left the thin lips.

Again the man in the blue jersey shuffled uneasily. 'There was a bit of trouble,' he muttered reluctantly. 'The pay wasn't too good, and the captain was a bit careless in leavin' things about — '

'And you helped yourself. I see!' The old man nodded quickly. 'And you've been working the river ever since?'

'That's right. Though there ain't many pickin's, what with one thing and another.'

'Show me what you've got,' broke in the man at the table abruptly.

The waterman fished in a pocket of his dungarees and produced a discoloured handkerchief knotted into a bundle. Setting it down on the table, he began laboriously to untie the knot.

'There y'are,' he said presently when

the contents of the handkerchief lay exposed. 'They ought to be worth a tenner.'

The old man stretched out a gloved hand and pulled the miscellaneous collection of objects towards him. In silence, he turned over the little heap of odd jewellery and grunted disparagingly.

'Two pounds!' he said. 'That's all it's worth to me.'

'Two pounds? Why, that there ring is worth more than that!'

'Two pounds!' repeated the old man. 'You can take it or leave it!'

'You're robbin' yourself, ain't you?' said the river thief sarcastically. 'Why, lummy, them two diamonds is worth more'n a tenner alone!'

'See here, my friend.' The voice of the old man at the table was cold and incisive. 'I never bargain. I've made you an offer, and if you'd like to accept it you can. If you don't, you can tie those things up — ' He jerked his head contemptuously at the contents of the handkerchief. ' — and take them away.'

'Make it a fiver,' pleaded the waterman, but the other shook his bald head.

'Two pounds, I said! And I'm not paying a penny more!'

Limmer sighed. 'It's sheer blinkin' robbery!' he protested. 'All right, hand over your two quid!'

One of the black-gloved hands disappeared into the pocket of the worn overcoat. There was a crackling rustle, and then the fingers reappeared holding two treasury notes. 'Here you are.'

The waterman took them, spat on them, and stowed them carefully away in his trouser pocket.

'You find working the river precarious?' asked the man at the table as he began to pack up the little heap of miscellaneous jewellery which he had just acquired.

'Precarious!' The waterman gave a short laugh. 'It's starvation. What with night watchmen and the police, a fellow don't get a chance.'

The old man looked at him steadily. 'How would you like a chance?' he said. 'Instead of being a freelance, how would you like to act under orders; a fixed salary and a periodical bonus?'

Limmer frowned. 'What d'you mean?'

'I'll tell you.' The old man leaned forward and rested his elbows on the table top. 'There's money to be picked up on the river, but not by the likes of you working on your own. You and river rats like you haven't got the brains to go out for the big money; but if you're willing to obey orders, to do as you're told and carry out my instructions, there's a good living for you, and very little risk. You'll get a fixed weekly salary and a bonus after every job, if you join the River Men.'

'I've 'eard of them,' said Limmer slowly. 'They were the fellows what cleared the *Contessa* of 'er cargo of whisky a week or two back. Got away with it under the noses of the river cops.'

'Your information is accurate,' murmured the bald-headed man. 'And every man concerned in that raid got a fiver bonus.'

The waterman stared at him, his eyes alight. 'I'm on, guv'nor!' he exclaimed. 'What do I do?'

The old man took a pencil and a scrap of paper from his pocket and rapidly scribbled something. 'Report at this address the day after tomorrow at six

11

o'clock. Ask for Joe Hickman. Remember the name, Joe Hickman. Say you want to go downstream with the ebb tide. He'll understand.'

He held out the scrap of paper and the man in the blue jersey took it, frowning at the scribbled line of pencilled writing. 'Ask for Joe Hickman,' he mumbled, 'and say I want to go downstream on the ebb tide.'

'That's right,' said the old man with a nod. 'He'll do the rest. And remember one thing — when you belong to the River Men, you do as you're told. Orders are to be obeyed implicitly.'

'Whose orders?' asked Limmer.

'Mine! I pay well and I expect service. If at any time you contemplate disobeying an order, just remember Lew Banning and think better of it.'

'Banning?' muttered Limmer. 'They took 'im out of the river a week ago.'

'He thought he was cleverer than I was, and . . . he went downstream on the ebb tide.'

The waterman stared at him, fascinated.

'Just remember,' went on the old man, 'that my word is law, and there'll be no trouble. I've got many people working under me, but I'm the boss. Don't forget that.'

'I shan't forget it,' said Limmer, and there was a subtle change in his voice. 'It's the one thing I wanted to know.' His right hand came quickly out of his dingy trousers. 'I want you, Mr. Unknown!' he said grimly. 'I'm Inspector Pelton of the river police, and I've been trying to locate you for six months!'

The figure at the table sat rigid, his eyes fixed on the automatic that was covering him.

'It's taken me a long time to find you,' went on Pelton, 'but I've got you at last!'

'You think so!' The words came out in a long-drawn hiss from between clenched teeth, and then suddenly, without warning, the gloved hands which had been gripping the edge of the table moved. The heavy mass of wood was flung forward and, overturning, caught Pelton painfully across the knees. He staggered, and before he could recover his balance, the figure of the old man had launched itself upon him.

Pelton fired twice, but the bullets went wide, burying themselves harmlessly in the wooden flooring. One of the gloved hands caught his pistol wrist with surprising strength, and with a sharp twist sent the weapon flying from his grasp. He was hurled backwards and fell with a crash, his assailant on the top of him.

The candle had gone out with the overturning of the table, but the dawn had come, and sufficient of the grey light percolated through the dirty windows to enable him to see the distorted face of his adversary. Wildly he fought to gain the upper hand, but the strength of his opponent was phenomenal. One of the black-gloved hands had fastened on his throat, the fingers closing tighter and tighter until he felt his head swimming.

In an effort to loosen that deadly grip, he clawed at the face above him. To his horror and surprise it came away in his hand, a clammy substance like thin rubber. Pointed chin and yellow skin; bald head and fringe of grey hair; he held them in his nerveless fingers! He caught a glimpse of another face, a younger face, a face twisted with rage; and then the suffocating grip on his throat grew tighter and his senses fled . . .

The man made sure his victim was unconscious and staggered to his feet. For a moment he rested against the over-turned table, panting heavily; and then when he had regained his breath, he went back to the motionless form of the unconscious detective and made a rapid search of his pockets. The address which he had scribbled on the scrap of paper and the two pound-notes he thrust into the pocket of his overcoat, and then hurrying to a dark corner of the gloomy chamber, he returned staggering under the weight of a long length of a rusty chain.

Working swiftly, he wound it carefully about the legs and body of Pelton, and when he had finished he straightened up, went over to the trap and opened it. He caught a glimpse of brown surging water on which the little dinghy rose and fell unevenly. Dragging the chained man over to the open trap, he pushed him

15

cautiously over the edge.

There was a dull splash as he fell into the running water. Below that turgid stream was six feet of glutinous Thames mud, and the chain was heavy . . .

The rope ladder was fastened to staples in the flooring near the trap, and he kicked it through the aperture. Descending the swaying structure until he was able to reach the ring to which the boat was tethered, he untied the painter and turned it adrift. Its nose caught in one of the piles and it swung half round; an eddy caught it and righted it, and it passed out of sight, heading downstream on the ebb tide.

The murderer returned to the gloomy chamber of the warehouse, pulled up the rope ladder, and closed the trap.

The sky in the east was pink when a man walked rapidly along Thames Street in the direction of Creek Bridge, leaving behind him the desolate bulk of Gallows Wharf, deserted now except for the rats which came cautiously out in the gloomy room above the river to nibble at the rotting grain, timidly at first, and then with increasing boldness as they realized that they were the sole occupants of the deserted building.

2

The House of Macintyre

On the Surrey shore of the river, midway between the foreign cattle market and the South Metropolitan Gas Works, stood an imposing warehouse with one of the best wharf frontages on the Thames. It was erected in the days when the surrounding district presented a more rural appearance than at present, when the narrow streets were flower-decked lanes and Deptford was, for the most part, green fields and meadows in which cattle grazed contentedly.

Here to the long wharf came ships from all countries with crews of many nationalities: cargo boats, orange ships from Spain, big Dutch barges gaily coloured with their brown sails furled; for the firm of Macintyre and Sloan, shippers and importers, did a thriving trade, and in the world of commerce were regarded as important. There was no Sloan — no one of that name had been connected with the firm for the past fifty years — but the old title was retained, for it carried with it the hallmark of integrity.

Cheques bearing the signature of the present head of the business were honoured without question in many parts of the world, and for surprising amounts. Roy Hugh Macintyre, the last of the original family who had started the firm in the days when George III sat on the throne of England, had only recently come into the business. On the death of his uncle, old Robert Macintyre, nine months previously, he had come over from America to take charge. A youngish-looking man in the early forties with dark hair in which as yet no touch of grey had appeared, he had arrived unknown and unheralded to the surprise of the staff, who until the death of their former employer had been unaware of his existence.

There had been some sort of trouble in the Macintyre family. Old Robert's brother had been something of a black sheep. Refusing to settle down to the business which his forefathers had founded, he had emigrated to America at an early age. Here for many years he had contrived to obtain a precarious livelihood. The final rupture between himself and his family occurred when he met and married an American woman, an actress in a road show.

When the news reached old Robert Macintyre, he wrote a stiff letter expressing his disapproval and refusing to hold any communication with one who, in his own words, 'had brought disgrace on an ancient and honourable family.'

A stubborn man with all the dour obstinacy of his race, he kept his word. His brother's wife died in giving birth to a son, and five years later, Hugh Macintyre was killed in a railroad accident. The boy, Roy Hugh Macintyre, was brought up by his mother's family, and his existence was undreamed of by old Robert till a year before his death. Many were the speculations among the staff concerning the new head of the firm prior to his arrival, and the general conclusion was that no one who had not been brought up in the business would be able to control the intricate ramifications of Macintyre and Sloan.

In this they were wrong, for Roy Hugh Macintyre exhibited an uncanny business ability, and before he had been in occupation of the shabby office very long from which his uncle had conducted the business for so many years, he had not only grasped the routine of the business but had suggested and put into practice a number of useful improvements.

Certainly he owed a lot, as he was the first to admit, to the help and experience of the general manager. James Swann, with the exception of one aged clerk, was the oldest member of the staff, and his knowledge of the business was encyclopaedic. In later years, when old Robert had been showing signs of the final break-up which had culminated in his death, Jimmy S, as he was affectionately known, had taken much of the work from his shoulders, and was in fact quite capable of running the business himself. A neat, good-humoured man, always ready with a word of encouragement for the lowliest employee, his thin, wiry figure was a familiar one in the vicinity of Butcher Road, in which the offices of Macintyre and Sloan had their main entrance.

Catherine Lee was a particular favourite of his. When she had first joined the firm as Robert Macintyre's private secretary, Jimmy S had gone out of his way to make her comfortable, and since that day had shown her many little kindnesses. She was thinking of Jimmy Swan as she sat at her worn desk in the small room adjoining Roy Macintyre's private office, which was reserved for her use. The little bunch of violets and primroses that occupied a broken vase in front of her could only have been put there by his hands. He was always doing things like that. Once, in his hearing, she had expressed a liking for a certain form of small cake, and the following day a plate of the pastries had been sent up with her afternoon cup of tea. As she sat there with the morning sun streaming through the window, she looked as unfitted to her surroundings as did the spring flowers in the cracked glass bowl.

There used to be an American artist, now dead, who specialized in a particular type of womanhood, and Catherine might have sat as a model for any one of the long series of pictures that had made his name world famous. She was slim without being thin, and beneath her fair complexion was a golden glow that is more often seen in Spanish women, which enhanced the redness of her lips and acted as a complement to her honey-coloured hair. Her eyes were large and grey and thoughtful, and looked steadily from beneath level brows. There was intelligence in her broad forehead and character in the firmness of her small mouth and rounded chin.

There was a tap at the door, and she looked up with a smile as the object of her thoughts came in.

'Good morning, Miss Lee,' said James Swann, the eyes behind his horn-rimmed spectacles twinkling. 'Getting used to the changed conditions?'

She nodded, looking at him critically. She thought he looked tired and harassed this morning, and older than usual. How old he really was she had often speculated, but come to no satisfactory conclusion. Jimmy S was one of those men whose age it was difficult to guess. He might have been anything between forty-five and sixty. There were no lines on his full, florid face, and only a tinge of grey in the dark hair that was brushed so carefully over his small head.

'I've brought those German bills of lading,' he said, laying some papers on her desk. 'Mr. Macintyre will want to see them. Has he come in yet?'

'I don't think so,' she answered. 'He hadn't a quarter of an hour ago when I looked into his office.'

He removed his glasses and polished them carefully with a silk handkerchief which he took from his breast pocket. 'How do you get on with him?' he asked.

'Fairly well,' she replied. 'Of course, he's different from old Mr. Macintyre.'

'Very,' agreed Jimmy S, replacing his spectacles on the bridge of his thin nose. 'I've never met a man so full of vitality and energy. Sometimes I wish he had a little less,' he added ruefully. 'He requires a lot of keeping pace with.'

She smiled in sympathy. The new head of the firm was certainly a worker. Without actually slacking, a great number of the staff had not put their full energies into the business under the regime of their late employer, and Roy Macintyre had been quick to see this and put his finger on the delinquents. There had been a general tightening up, particularly in the counting-house, where the long rows of clerks had been used to taking life more or less easily.

'Yes, he requires a lot of living up to,' repeated Jimmy S thoughtfully, 'but I think under his guidance the business will improve. It needed bucking up.'

'Have you any interest outside the business?' she asked quizzically, and he laughed.

'I've spent forty years of my life, man and boy, in the service of Macintyre and Sloan,' he replied. 'What other interests should I have?'

The buzzer rang before she could

answer, and picking up pencil and note-book and the documents he had brought her, she went over to the communicating door, and after a preliminary tap, entered.

The new head of Macintyre and Sloan sat behind his broad desk reading a letter. He had evidently only just come in, for the majority of his correspondence which she had placed on his blotting-pad was as yet unopened. He glanced up as she entered, gave a curt nod and went on reading the letter. Catherine waited, a little uncomfortably. For some reason which she could never fathom, she always felt ill at ease in the presence of this man. It may have been his manner, for without being rude he was abrupt, and treated her more as a machine than a human being.

'I have some instructions for the packing department,' he said abruptly. 'Take them, will you?'

Almost before she was ready, he began to dictate rapidly in the curious mixture of Scottish and American accents that was one of his chief peculiarities.

'Have that typed at once,' he said when he had finished, 'and post it up in the packing department. What are those papers you've got there?'

She laid the bills of lading before him, and he glanced through them quickly.

'All right, I'll attend to these later,' he said. 'I shall have some letters for you in twenty minutes.'

He picked up a paper-knife from the desk beside him with a nod of dismissal, and she was turning away when a knock came at the door and Swann entered apologetically.

'There's a man wishes to see you, sir — ' he began, but his employer interrupted him.

'I can't see anyone!' he snapped shortly, his dark brows contracting. 'You know I never make appointments before eleven.'

'This man is from the river police,' said the manager. 'Inspector Terry Ward, and he said that his business was urgent.'

Catherine could have sworn that the sallow face of Macintyre went a shade paler.

'The police?' he said. 'What do the police want with me?'

'He wouldn't state his business. He said it was important that he should see you.'

Macintyre's frown deepened, and he pursed his thin lips. 'All right,' he said grudgingly. 'Send him up. Get that notice typed at once, Miss Lee; I want it posted in the packing room as soon as possible. Just a minute, Swann,' he added, as the manager was on the point of taking his departure. 'I'd like a word with you.'

Catherine left them together, and she was typing furiously when the unwelcome caller was shown into her little office.

Inspector Terry Ward of the Thames Police was not at all the type of man she had expected. He was tall, with a brown, attractive face, a face tanned by constant exposure to many weathers. He carried his hat in his hand, and his close-cropped hair was brown with a wave in it that no amount of brushing had succeeded in eradicating. If the truth must be told, this wave was one of Terry Ward's greatest burdens. For years he had tried every conceivable method of removing it, but without success, for it was a conviction of his that wavy hair in a man was effeminate, and permissible only in the case of band leaders, film stars and actors whose living depended more or less on their attractiveness to the opposite sex.

'Good morning,' he said pleasantly. 'I hope I'm not intruding, but I was sent up here to wait until Mr. Macintyre could see me.'

He had a deep, not unmusical voice, and his broad smile showed a set of even, very white teeth.

'I don't think Mr. Macintyre will keep you very long,' said Catherine. 'Won't you sit down?' She glanced at the only other chair the office contained, but he shook his head.

'I'd rather stand, if you don't mind,' he said. 'I'm used to standing.' There was frank admiration in his eyes as he looked at her, and she coloured. To hide her discomposure, she returned to her typing, and he strolled over to the window and stood looking out onto the river.

After a few moments James Swann came out of the inner office and paused at Catherine's desk on his way to the door. 'Mr. Macintyre will see Inspector Ward now, Miss Lee,' he said, and with a nod to the waiting man, went out.

Catherine rose to her feet. 'Will you come this way, Mr. Ward,' she said, and the young inspector followed her as she led the way to the door of Roy Macintyre's private sanctum. Ushering him in, she closed the door behind him and returned to her work.

Leaning back in his chair, Macintyre regarded his visitor across the broad desk coldly. 'What is the important matter you wish to see me about, Inspector?' he asked.

Terry returned his gaze without flinching. 'In the early hours of this morning,' he said, 'the warehouse belonging to Messrs. Woodhouse and Selhurst, near East India Dock, was broken into, the night watchman bludgeoned to death, and twenty-four cases of cigars stolen.'

Roy Macintyre raised his eyebrows. 'That's very interesting, Inspector,' he said, 'but I fail to see what it has to do with me.'

'It has this to do with you, sir,' said Terry Ward curtly, and thrusting his hand in his breast pocket he pulled out a small leather notecase. 'This was found beneath the dead body of the watchman,' he went on sternly, 'and your name is stamped in gold letters on the inner flap! I should like you to explain how it got there.'

3

Concerning the River Men

Without any outward sign of discomposure, Roy Macintyre leaned forward and
stretched out a hand. 'May I see that?' he
asked coolly.

Rather reluctantly, Terry gave him the
small leather case. Macintyre examined it
carefully, looked at the embossed name
on the flap, and nodded.

'This is, without a doubt, mine,' he
admitted. 'But how it came to be found in
the place you mentioned, I cannot imagine. Of course, you're not for a moment
suggesting that I had anything to do with
the death of this man, and the robbery at
Woodhouse and Selhurst's?'

'I'm not suggesting anything, Mr.
Macintyre,' answered the inspector. 'I'm
merely following up an inquiry.'

'Yes, of course, very properly. Well, I
can only tell you, Inspector, that I've

given up using this notecase for some considerable time. I found it was inadequate for my needs and bought another.' He took from his pocket a Russia leather wallet, bound with gold corners, and exhibited it to Terry. 'This is the one I've been using for the past two months.'

'What did you do with the other one?' asked the inspector.

Macintyre shook his head. 'I'm rather careless about things I've discarded. I suppose I must have left it lying about somewhere.'

It was an unsatisfactory explanation. Something of his feelings must have shown in Terry's face, for Macintyre went on quickly: 'I'm sorry I can't be of more assistance, Inspector, but there it is.' He tossed the little notecase across the desk towards the young inspector with a gesture that was intended to signify that the interview was over; but Terry had other views.

'I wish you could be a little more explicit, Mr. Macintyre,' he said, picking up the case. 'Can't you possibly remember what you did with this when you

33

bought the new one?'

Macintyre leaned back in his chair, half closing his eyes in an effort of memory. 'No,' he answered presently, 'I can't. I must have put it somewhere, but I can't remember where.'

'You realize how important it is?' urged Terry. 'It's obvious that this case was in the possession of one of the men who were responsible for the robbery and murder of the watchman. Which means that in some way they must have got hold of it after you'd finished using it.'

'I quite realize that,' said Macintyre, 'but I can't help you any more than I have done. It's possible I may have left it at my flat, or maybe this office.'

'Which do you consider more likely?'

Macintyre shrugged his shoulders. 'I've already told you, I don't know.'

'Wherever you left it, it would seem that someone had stolen it.'

'That is evident,' answered the other dryly, 'for I can assure you, Inspector, it was not I who dropped it at Woodhouse and Selhurst's.'

Terry fingered his chin uncertainly. If

Macintyre was speaking the truth concerning the little case, its usefulness as a clue to the perpetrator of the robbery was considerably decreased. On the other hand, it struck him that were Macintyre concerned with the theft of the cigars and the murder of the watchman, his explanation was one of the best he could have offered.

'Supposing,' he said, 'that you'd left this at your house, who'd be in a position to get hold of it?'

Macintyre took a thin platinum case from his pocket and helped himself to a cigarette. 'Quite a number of people. I spend very little of my time at home, and the flat is looked after by a man and his wife who attend to my needs. There's no knowing who they might admit during my absence.'

'Have you always found them trustworthy?'

Macintyre struck a match and lit the cigarette that drooped from his thin lips. 'Naturally. Otherwise they wouldn't still be in my employ. But I can't vouch for anyone they might admit, or who might, on some pretext or another, gain admission.'

Terry was forced to see the truth of this. 'And what about this office? Supposing you had left the case here?'

'It would be easier for anyone to get hold of it here than at my flat. A great number of people are passing in and out all day, and I'm sometimes away for several hours.'

Terry put several further questions, but when he took his leave a few minutes later, he had acquired nothing that added to his slender stock of knowledge concerning the leather notecase found beneath the dead body of the watchman.

He made his way across the busy wharf to where the police launch in which he had come was moored, and stepped on board. The engineer, who was also the steersman, looked at him inquiringly.

'Make for Waterloo Float,' said Terry, and he seated himself in the stern.

The launch moved away from the wharf and headed upstream. There was a conference at the Yard that morning to which he had been invited, and during the journey Terry's mind was fully occupied with the unsatisfactory result of his recent interview and his forthcoming discussion with his superiors.

Terry had joined the Thames Police, which had the distinction of being the oldest branch of the Metropolitan Force, at the end of the war. During that period, he had served as a temporary lieutenant in the Royal Navy, and his rank had assisted him considerably in gaining his rapid promotion. A small private income inherited from his father, who had been a captain in the Mercantile Marine, was insufficient to provide him with anything but the bare necessities of life, and looking round at the conclusion of hostilities for something that would augment this microscopic competence, he had chosen the river police, partly because he liked an open-air life, and partly because such a career offered just the spice of excitement that his adventurous soul craved. Terry Ward was not the type of man who could settle down to an office work. That he had a flair for his job was quickly proved by the rapid way in which he had risen from the ranks to his present position.

The Thames Police was a small body compared with their land brothers, for it consisted of only two hundred men; but in spite of its smallness, it was a very important section of the Metropolitan Police Force which ensured law and order and guarded the property of the people. During the course of any given year, hundreds of millions of pounds' worth of merchandise entered the Port of London from all over the earth, and but for the vigilance of the men who patrolled the river unceasingly by day and night, a great portion of these riches would have found their way into the greedy hands of the river thieves. Before the advent of the Thames Police, London's waterway had been infested by pirates and thieves who had robbed vessels big and small, their loot running into thousands of pounds weekly.

The disposal of these stolen goods was easy enough, for even up to a few years ago the banks of the Thames had been crowded with fences who received all stolen property and paid cut-throat rates, waxing rich and fat from the profits of their nefarious dealings. Thanks to the efficiency of the men whose duty it was to keep the river free of these pests, both thieves and fences were now as scarce as strawberries in mid-winter. The ceaseless vigilance of the patrols, silent and watchful in their little small-oared boats or, when speed was important, powerful motor-launches, had made the activities of these river rats a hazardous and unprofitable occupation. Many was the unfortunate, too, who owed his life to these men, for the Thames provided a great attraction for the would-be suicide. In sunlight and shadow, in rain and fog, the river police were always on duty, nosing in and out of clustered shipping, exchanging friendly greetings with the people they knew, and keeping a searching lookout for all suspicious characters. Many a lonely watchman was cheered by the friendly hail of the keen-eyed men as they passed in the silence of the night, and the most daring of the river thieves slinked into his lair at their approach.

The launch passed through the Pool, threading its way among innumerable craft, came eventually to Blackfriars Bridge, and drawing into the Embankment side, presently slowed up at the floating police station. A Thames policeman caught the painter skilfully and tied it up. Terry stepped ashore, exchanged a greeting with the sergeant in charge, and making his way up the steps came out on to the Embankment. Crossing the road, he walked swiftly towards the entrance to Scotland Yard, and passing under the arch entered the vestibule of that gloomy building.

In the big conference room he found six men already seated at one end of the long table. Near the thin-faced Chief Inspector Ransom was a vacant chair, and in this Terry seated himself.

'Now that you've come, Ward, we can get on with the matter in hand,' said a grey-haired chief constable at the head of the table. He flicked open a folder in front of him and glanced at the typewritten notes and reports that it contained, although he had seen them many times and knew most of them by heart. 'There is, without a doubt,' he went on, 'a new organization operating on the river. We've had proof of that for the past six months, and something must be done immediately to check their activities.'

'We're doing all we can, sir,' said Terry.

The chief constable made an impatient gesture. 'I know, I know!' he said curtly. 'But it's results we want, Ward. Have you discovered anything further concerning the disappearance of Pelton?'

Terry shook his head. 'No, sir. Pelton disappeared a month ago, and no trace of him has been found since.'

'According to a report you made at the time,' said Chief Inspector Ransom, 'Pelton was hopeful of discovering something concerning this organization which has come into being. Isn't that so?'

'Yes, sir. He told me that he thought he'd got a clue that would lead him to the man at the head of it. That was the last time I saw him.'

'It seems,' put in the quiet voice of Superintendent Wingarb, 'that he was speaking the truth. It looks very much as

41

if he had followed up this clue he mentioned and found trouble. There can be no explanation for his non-appearance other than that he was murdered and his body weighted and sunk in the river.'

'I'm afraid you're right, sir,' agreed Terry. 'That's my own conclusion.'

'The whole question is,' said the chief constable, 'what's to be done? It's quite obvious that we're dealing with some clever man who's succeeded in organizing the river thieves. Incredible as it may sound, the evidence we've received during the past eight or nine months is capable of no other interpretation.' He searched among the papers in front of him and drew out a long typewritten list. 'Beginning with last July,' he went on, 'we have twenty-seven cases of warehouse and factory robberies on the banks of the river between the Pool and Erith. Fifteen cargo-broaching complaints, and seven cases of murder! Not for the past fifty years has there been such an outbreak of thieving and crime on the river, and in not one single instance has the thief or thieves been apprehended, nor any clue to their identity discovered. There's something wrong somewhere.' He shook his head disapprovingly.

Terry was silent. He could offer no defence to the chief constable's reprimand.

'I suppose you're taking every possible precaution, Ward?' said Superintendent Wingarb.

'I'm doing everything I can, sir,' answered Terry. 'The patrols in Greenwich Reach, Rotherhithe and Wapping have been doubled, and every known river thief and suspected fence has been subjected to a close questioning, but without result. I'm quite prepared to admit that so far we've been beaten. I thought in this last outrage at Woodhouse and Selhurst's that we'd discovered an important clue, but it led nowhere. At least, it hasn't at present.' Briefly he gave an account of the finding of the notecase and the result of his interview of the morning.

'Hm!' said the chief constable when he had finished. 'Do you know anything about this man Macintyre?'

'Only that he came over from America eight months ago to take charge of his uncle's business,' replied Terry.

'Eight months ago, eh?' said Chief Inspector Ransom quickly. 'That's just about the time this new river ramp started.'

'It may be a coincidence,' grunted Wingarb. 'On the other hand,' finished the chief constable, 'it may not. The thing that has been so puzzling to us is how the thieves succeeded in getting away with the goods. You say you're confident they don't use the river, Inspector?' He looked across at Terry, and the latter nodded.

'I'm practically sure they don't, sir,' he answered. 'We've kept a sharp lookout for any suspicious craft, and we've seen nothing.'

'Our own men have had instructions to watch for any suspicious vehicles in the vicinity of the riverbank,' said Ransom, 'and their reports have been negative.'

The chief constable leaned back wearily in his chair. 'Are you suggesting that they get the stuff away by air?' he asked sarcastically. 'That's the only alternative you appear to have left. It isn't as if they confined themselves to goods that are easily portable, such as currency or jewellery. In the case of the *Contessa*, they stole a whole cargo of whisky after clubbing the night watchman into unconsciousness. When they broke into the warehouse of Gilling and Hill, they took forty thousand pounds' worth of silk. In the case of last night's robbery, twenty-four cases of cigars were stolen; and I could give you a score of other instances. All these things were bulky and not easily removable. How did they succeed in getting them away?'

Terry shook his head. 'I can only repeat, sir, that it wasn't by way of the river. I've questioned all the patrols that were out last night, and no boat that could possibly have been used for the removal of the cases from Woodhouse and Selhurst's was seen.'

'It looks to me,' said Wingarb thoughtfully, 'as if this man Macintyre, whom you interviewed this morning, Ward, would be worth watching. Apart from the method by which these people succeed in getting their loot away, they must have a pretty good distributing centre. You can't dispose of forty thousand pounds' worth of silk, for instance, through the ordinary fencing channels. But it wouldn't be difficult to do so through a reputable firm like Macintyre and Sloan.'

'There's a lot of truth in that, Wingarb,' said the chief constable. 'Their reputation is irreproachable, and the facilities a firm like that would have for getting the stuff out of the country are innumerable. I think it's a good suggestion.'

'I'll attend to it, sir,' said Terry, who had already decided on a similar plan, but was wise enough not to say so. 'I'll have a close watch kept from now on.'

'I think you may learn something,' said Wingarb. 'There are two ways of tackling this business. One is to discover how the stuff is fenced, and the other is to find out how they succeed in getting it away.'

'And the most important thing,' interjected Ransom, 'is to discover who the man is at the head of affairs. I know something of these river rats; they're incapable of planning anything for themselves. He's the fellow we want to lay our hands on. Once we get him, the whole organization will collapse like a house of cards.'

They discussed the matter in detail and from all angles, and it was two o'clock before Terry Ward left the Yard and went back to his waiting launch.

On the return journey to his headquarters at Wapping, his thoughts turned to the woman he had met that morning. Catherine Lee had created an impression that would have astonished her, had she been aware of it; and for the greater part of the time which the speedy launch took to cover the distance to Wapping Stairs, Terry sought for a plausible excuse that would enable him to meet her again.

The boat reached its destination before he found one; and had he but known it, an excuse was not necessary, for he was to meet Catherine Lee again very shortly and in circumstances which even his wildest imaginings could not have pictured.

4

Mr. Macintyre Receives a Visitor

The last of the staff had long since gone when Roy Macintyre closed the little book he had been studying, replaced it in his pocket, and rising from his desk, stretched himself. Putting on his hat and coat, he locked his desk, passed out of his office, and closing the door behind him, locked that also. Without haste, he made his way down the dark and narrow stairs that led to the ground floor. In the vestibule, the timekeeper wished him good night, to which he replied rather curtly and passed on, descending the steps to where his car awaited him.

The brightness of the day had given place to a thin, wetting drizzle, and he was glad to step into the warm interior of the saloon after a murmured order to his chauffeur. The car moved forward, rolled smoothly through the big gates into

Butcher Road, and turned into Watergate Street.

Roy Macintyre lit a cigarette, and settling himself comfortably against the padded cushions, allowed his thoughts to dwell on the events of the day as the car sped through the drabness of Deptford towards the West End. Although he had given no outward sign, the advent of Terry Ward had been something of a shock, and the uneasiness which he had experienced at the inspector's visit was still with him. It was impossible that the man should suspect anything, but it had been an unpleasant experience. That the wallet had been found where it had was a piece of bad luck. Without that, there was nothing to bring him in contact with the law.

He sat hunched up in the corner of the saloon, staring through the windows at the wet and shiny streets. Nobody knew better than he the risk he was running, and yet the reward was worth it. Big money had always attracted him, but until recently there had been little hope of it coming his way. Now, provided he went cautiously and avoided the pitfalls that strewed his path on every side, he would very soon be a rich man.

He allowed his thoughts to dally with the pleasant prospect which the future offered, and it was with a start that he realized that the car had stopped outside the entrance to his flat.

Getting out, he gave his chauffeur instructions for the morning and passed into the vestibule. A uniformed porter sitting in a glass cubbyhole by the wide staircase smiled a greeting which Macintyre barely acknowledged. Crossing to the automatic lift, he entered the little cage, closed the grill, and pressing a button was rapidly carried up to the fourth floor. Stepping out on to the spacious landing, he walked across to one of the two polished doors that faced each other, and taking a key from his pocket, let himself in.

The appointments of the flat were luxurious. Persian rugs covered the polished floor of the hall, and from the centre of the glossy ceiling hung a silver lamp that shed a soft glow over the gleaming paintwork. Macintyre removed his hat and coat, hung them on a carved stand of inlaid ebony, and went into his study. Here there was more evidence of wealth and taste. The carpet which covered the floor was of so thick a pile that it was like walking on a well-kept lawn. Low bookcases of Macassar ebony and polished sycamore occupied three walls of the oblong apartment. A big desk of the same woods faced the door, and in front of the silver electric radiator stood several deep, comfortable-looking leather chairs. Pressing a bell by the side of the mantelpiece, Macintyre dropped into one of the chairs and stretched his legs towards the glowing warmth of the fire.

In answer to his ring, the door opened noiselessly, and a small thin man in the conventional garb of a servant entered.

'Bring me a cocktail and the evening paper, Mint,' ordered Macintyre, and the little man bowed and withdrew as silently as he had appeared.

Flicking open a silver box on a low table at his elbow, Macintyre helped himself to a cigarette and smoked thoughtfully, staring at the ceiling. His plans had been carefully laid. So far as he could see there was no danger, and yet he wanted to make sure.

Mint returned, carrying a selection of evening newspapers in one hand and a silver tray on which stood a small glass in the other. Arranging the papers near his master's hand, he carefully set down the glass and straightened up.

'Dinner will be ready in three quarters of an hour, sir,' he said in the soft voice of the perfect servant.

Macintyre, in the act of opening one of the papers, nodded, and then, as the servant was crossing to the door: 'I'm expecting someone to call. A man is coming to see me on business. If I haven't finished dinner when he arrives, show him in here.'

'Yes, sir.' Mint bowed and withdrew.

Rapidly, Macintyre skimmed through the papers. The account of the warehouse robbery and the murder of the night watchman occupied a double-column spread on the front page, and this he read carefully, sipping meanwhile at his cocktail. When he had finished both the news and the drink, he got up, crossed the hall to his bedroom and rapidly dressed. As he finished tying his tie, the silver note of a gong warned him that his meal was ready.

Going into his cosy dining-room, he took his place at the oval table and leisurely proceeded to enjoy the excellent dinner that his cook-housekeeper had prepared for him. He was nibbling a biscuit and cheese when the soft whir of the bell reached his ears. A few minutes later he heard the murmur of voices, the gentle thud of the front door closing and the click of the study lock. There was a tap on the door of the dining-room, and Mint appeared.

'The — er — the gentleman has arrived, sir,' he said.

'Take my coffee into the study,' said Macintyre, 'and bring some whisky and soda.'

The servant went out, closing the door, and after a minute or two Macintyre got up, dusted the crumbs from his waistcoat with his napkin, tossed it on to the table by the side of his plate, and made his way to his study.

The man, who was standing straddle-legged in front of the fire, looked up as he entered. He was a thick-set, red-faced individual dressed in a cheap suit of blue serge which had obviously been bought ready-made. His plump hands were none too clean, and the nails were coarse and broken.

'Good evening, Mr. Macintyre,' he said in a husky voice. 'Nice little place you've got here.'

'It has its advantages,' said Macintyre coldly. 'Sit down, Copping.' He jerked his head towards one of the easy chairs, and going over to the big desk settled himself in the padded chair behind it. 'Now,' he said when his visitor was also seated, 'you've done what I told you?'

'Yes, Mr. Macintyre,' said Copping. 'The stuff'll arrive on Wednesday of next week. It's coming as a consignment of bricks from Belgium.'

Macintyre took his little notebook from his pocket and made a brief entry. 'Now, what about its disposal?' he said.

Copping plunged a fat hand into his breast pocket and withdrew a sheaf of crumpled papers. Spreading these out on a broad knee, he searched through them, finally selecting two, which he took over to the man at the desk. ''Ere y'are,' he said. 'You'll find all you want there.'

Mint came in at that moment with coffee and the whisky, and no further word was spoken until he had withdrawn.

'Help yourself,' said Macintyre, nodding towards the tray; and while Copping poured himself out a generous whisky and soda, he examined the papers that the other had placed before him. 'These seem all right,' he said. 'I suppose you can vouch for them?'

'You bet your life I can,' said Copping, smacking his lips and setting down his half-empty glass. 'They knows the ropes.'

Macintyre drank his coffee and pushed aside the cup and saucer. 'You clearly understand,' he said, 'that I'm not connected with this in any way. If there's any kick coming, it comes to you. There's nothing whatever to connect me with this business.'

'Sure, that's understood,' broke in Copping. 'Isn't that what we agreed on?

You needn't worry, Mr. Macintyre; there'll be no kick coming your way. None of these fellows know you, and few of them know me. I'm working mostly through intermediaries.' He gulped the remainder of his drink and picked up the decanter.

'I shouldn't have too much of that stuff,' warned Macintyre. 'It's dangerous, if you want to keep your wits about you.'

Copping chuckled throatily. 'I could drink a gallon of this stuff and not turn an 'air,' he said boastingly. 'The whisky ain't been distilled yet that could make me drunk. Why, I remember once . . . ' He told a story that made up in coarseness for what it lacked in humour.

'You may have a head like cast iron,' said Macintyre, 'but the less you drink while you're mixed up in this business, the better. Pull your chair up here and listen while I tell you my plans.'

Copping obeyed, his refilled glass in his hand; and for the greater part of an hour Roy Macintyre talked rapidly, referring every now and again to the little book which was open before him on the desk. He spoke almost uninterruptedly, for his listener only occasionally interjected a remark, contenting himself most of the time with an affirmatory nod of the head at the end of each staccato sentence that fell from the other's lips.

'There ain't no flies on you,' he remarked admiringly when Macintyre had finished outlining his scheme.

'No, I don't think there are,' agreed his host a trifle complacently. 'You think the idea is sound?'

'Sound!' exclaimed Copping. 'It's 'ide-bound and armour-plated, guv'nor. There ain't a flaw!'

'Well, it's up to you to carry it out.' Macintyre leaned back in his chair and looked at him steadily. 'Without any mistakes,' he added meaningfully.

'Mistakes?' echoed Copping. 'When Steve Copping does a thing, there ain't such things as mistakes. You ask anybody from Creek Bridge to Wapping Stairs and they'll tell you that there ain't a more reliable man alive than me.' He tapped his chest as he made this immodest assertion, and rising to his feet, poured out another drink. 'Won't you 'ave one?' he said. 'Come on, just to drink success to the partner-ship.'

'If I wanted to drink success, it would be in water!' snapped Macintyre coldly. 'You heed what I say, Copping, and go easy with that stuff.'

Copping tossed off the drink and put down the glass. 'I ain't 'ad enough to 'urt a child!' he protested.

'And get it out of your head that there's anything in the nature of a partnership between us,' went on Macintyre as though he hadn't spoken. 'I'm paying you, and paying you well for your services, and that's all there is to it!' His voice held the quality of steel in its tone, and his eyes were hard.

'No offence, Mr. Macintyre. It was only a figure of speech.'

'Well, erase the figure from your mind! There's no partnership between you and me, Copping. A business arrangement if you like, but no partnership.' He got up, and coming round the desk, took up a position in front of the glowing radiator. 'I think that's all we've got to discuss. You've got a telephone number that will always find me, but be careful what you say. If you talk about bricks I shall understand.'

Copping took the rather pointed hint and looked round for his hat; his overcoat he had kept on throughout the interview. 'Well, I'll be getting along, Mr. Macintyre,' he said. 'I'll fix all this up, don't you worry.'

'I'm not worrying. It's you who'll do the worrying — if you let me down.'

'You can bank on me. I ain't never let anybody down in me life.' He jammed his hat on his head and held out his hand, but ignoring it, Macintyre walked over to the door and opened it.

'Good night,' he said shortly. 'And don't forget what you've got to do.'

He stood on the threshold of the study until Mint had let his visitor out, and then going into his bedroom, he exchanged his dinner-suit for another one of shabby tweed. Coming back to the study, he called his servant.

'I'm going out,' he said. 'I don't know what time I shall be back. Don't wait up for me.'

'Very good, sir,' said Mint. 'It's a nasty night, raining like cats and dogs, sir. Do you want me to order you a taxi?'

'No, I'm not going very far. I'll walk.'

When he was alone, he poured himself out a small whisky and soda, and lighting a cigarette, stood leaning against the mantelpiece, staring thoughtfully at the red wires of the radiator. It was nearly half-past eleven when he roused himself, and going out into the hall, he opened a cupboard from which he took a shabby black overcoat and a soft hat. Putting these on, he left the flat and was carried swiftly down to the ground floor in the automatic lift. There was no night porter attached to the building in which he lived, and the day man had long since gone home to his well-earned rest, so there was no one to see him unfasten the heavy outer door and pass out into the almost deserted street. No one, that was, from within; the bored man who had been watching the building from the opposite side of the road for the greater part of the evening saw him come out, and as he hurried up the street through the falling rain, began to move cautiously in his wake.

Luckily for Roy Hugh Macintyre's peace of mind, he was unaware of the trailer who followed so close on his heels.

5

Joe Hickman

Mr. Copping came out of the warm atmosphere of Waverly Mansions into the cold wetness of the street, and cursed below his breath at the unpleasantness of the weather.

Macintyre's flat was situated in a quiet thoroughfare at the back of Piccadilly, and Mr. Copping's pale blue eyes looked in vain for a taxi. He was getting wet, and the longer he waited the wetter he was likely to become. Deciding after a few minutes that his best course would be to make for the main road, he turned up the collar of his coat and set off briskly. As he reached the corner, a taxi hove in sight and he hailed it. The driver brought the machine to the kerb with a scream of protesting brakes.

'Take me to the public library in Woolwich Road,' said Mr. Copping, jerking open the door, 'and get a move on, I'm in a hurry!' He stepped inside, ignoring the protest the cab-driver began to make.

The cab moved off. He settled himself back in a corner of the seat, and taking a packet of cigarettes from his pocket, lit one.

With the glowing cylinder of tobacco drooping from his thick lips, he gave himself up to his thoughts, and they centred round the man with whom he had had his recent interview. There was a fellow who had a good opinion of himself, thought Mr. Copping contemptuously; a fellow who treated a man like dirt. There was no denying he had brains — up to a point. But in some respects he was a fool — how great a fool he didn't realize. Only for the fact that he had private objects to serve, Mr. Copping would have given him a piece of his mind for trying to pull that servant stuff.

Removing the cigarette from his mouth, he allowed his lips to curl back in a snarl that showed his yellow teeth. Servant! Him! He'd show Mr. Haughty Blooming Macintyre one day who was the servant! His mind dwelt lovingly on that pleasant future. Who was he, anyhow, to grudge a man his drop of liquor? But what could you expect from a fellow with a name like Macintyre? Well, he'd come to his cuttings down, and in the meanwhile it didn't do any harm to humour him. There was money to be made, and the big fellow had certain plans of his own. He'd be seeing the big fellow later on that night to report.

He was a weird bloke; not all that he seemed by a long chalk. Mr. Copping would have liked to have known a great deal more about him, but on the only occasion that he had attempted to discover anything, he had received a scare that had effectually put a stop to his curiosity — at least, in any practical form. Clever, too; compared with his brain, Macintyre's was little better than a rabbit's.

Thinking of the big fellow, Mr. Copping became so engrossed in his thoughts that it was with a start of surprise that he realized the cab had reached its destination. With a hurried glance at the clock, he got out. As he reached in his pockets for the fare, the aged driver uttered his protest.

'This is a nice place to come,' he grumbled. 'I'll 'ave difficulty in getting a fare from 'ere back to the West End.'

'I bet you will,' said Mr. Copping unsympathetically. 'They don't go in for taxis in these parts.'

He dropped some coins into the man's hand and walked away, deaf to the indignant remarks of the driver as he discovered the smallness of his tip.

A hundred paces beyond the place where the cab had stopped was a side turning, a narrow, dark and uninviting street lit economically and lined with gloomy-looking tenement houses. Into this he turned and made his way to the end. Crossing a broader road, he negotiated a series of even less prepossessing streets until eventually he came to one running parallel with the river. The rain was still falling, but not so heavily, as he came to a halt outside a large brick building that bore in faded letters on the facia 'Hickman's Billiards Saloon'.

Ascending the shallow flight of broad

steps, Mr. Copping pushed open a glazed swing door and entered a shabby lobby. A man was seated behind a narrow counter in an alcove on the right reading a newspaper. He glanced up as Mr. Copping entered, and nodded. 'Good evening, Sam,' said Mr. Copping pleasantly. 'The guv'nor about?'

'He's in his office,' answered the man addressed as Sam.

'O.K.,' said Copping, and he walked over to a green baize door that faced the entrance. As he pushed it open, the click of balls came to his ears, and he found himself looking into a long, lofty room, through the smoke-laden atmosphere of which shone great green-shaded lamps suspended from the girdered roof, over a score of billiard tables that ran down either side. A mixed collection of men were grouped about these, playing snooker for the most part. Some of them were well dressed in a flashy way, others shabby and down at heel. There were weather-beaten men whose tanned faces proclaimed a life spent in the open; weedy youths, sallow and unhealthy-looking; men of all ages and types, with only one common quality — a certain shiftiness of eye that betrayed them to the skilled observer as all belonging to the genus Crook.

The building which housed Hickman's Saloon had originally been built as a mission hall for seamen, but in spite of the efforts of its sponsors, it failed to attract the men for whom it had been intended, these unregenerate souls preferring the more garish entertainment provided by the numerous public-houses of the district, and had fallen empty.

Joe Hickman had stepped in and acquired it from the disillusioned committee to whom it belonged for an absurdly low rental, had cleared out the rows of chairs and dismantled the platform from which well-meaning men and women had lectured to the handful of dazed sailors who had been induced to attend, installed billiard tables and opened it as a temperance billiard saloon, with instantaneous success. Word had quickly passed around the district that the inclusion of 'Temperance' in the title was more or less misleading. Regular customers and men known to the fat and genial proprietor could always get a drop of the right stuff at Hickman's. In consequence of this, the place quickly became popular, developing into a kind of club and general meeting-place for the men of the neighbourhood. Rumours spread that other things besides billiards could be played, and these rumours were not without foundation. There was a small room at the end of the long hall furnished with a dozen or more card tables, but only a chosen few among Mr. Hickman's patrons were aware of its existence.

The police suspected that less innocent amusements had their genesis at the billiard hall, but they had never been able to prove anything. Certain it was that it was frequented by thieves and vagabonds and the riff-raff of Woolwich and Rotherhithe, with occasionally a sprinkling of Wapping. Its situation, backing as it did on the river, was a great advantage in its proprietor's eyes, and many were the illicit deals that took place on the narrow strip of wharfage under cover of darkness between the owner and men who came furtively in small boats with muffled oars.

Mr. Copping gave a casual glance round the big room, acknowledged the greetings from one or two acquaintances who had looked round at his entrance, and made his way towards a narrow door in the left wall. At this he tapped, and in response to a growled invitation, entered.

The room beyond was small and not overly clean. The air was blue with smoke, and through the haze he saw the enormous figure of the man who sat in a padded chair behind the battered desk which occupied more than a third of the available space.

'Big' is a description which inadequately described Joe Hickman. He was colossal. A great fleshy mountain of a man, whose eyes were almost concealed by the puffy fatness of his cheeks, and whose loose-lipped mouth formed a vivid splash of colour against the leaden hue of his skin.

'Hello, Steve!' he said without removing the cigar which was clenched between his broken teeth. 'Sit down.'

His voice had a curious husky quality, as though he suffered from laryngitis, and in spite of the coldness of the night he was in his shirt sleeves, rolled up to reveal the muscular and hairy forearms. Copping pulled forward a rickety armchair and sank into it.

'Got anything to drink?' he asked. 'I'm thirsty.'

Mr. Hickman reached out a hand to a small cupboard in the wall beside him and produced a bottle and glasses. Splashing some of the spirit into them, he pushed one towards his visitor, and Copping drained it at a draught, smacking his lips with satisfaction.

'That's better,' he grunted. 'Well, any news?'

Mr. Hickman, twisting his glass between an enormous thumb and forefinger, and eyeing the swirling yellow liquid it contained, slowly shook his head. 'No, nothing fresh. You didn't expect anything, did you?'

'No, I just asked.'

'Maybe you'll hear something tonight. You're seeing *him* later, aren't you?'

Copping nodded. 'Yes. I got a telephone message this morning.'

'So did I. He told me to warn the boys

there'd be another job on in a day or two.'

'The more the merrier, so far as I'm concerned,' remarked Copping with a grin. 'We haven't done so badly, you know, Joe. During the last eight months, we've cleared a nice little bit.'

'Yes, might do worse. Though I'm not at all satisfied, personally.'

'Why, what's wrong?' asked Copping quickly.

'There's nothing wrong, but . . . well, I'd like to know more about this fellow.' Mr. Hickman poured the contents of the glass down his throat, looked at it, and set it on the desk. 'I'd like to know who he is and all about him. It's all very well, you know, Steve; we're making a nice little packet at present. But if anything goes wrong, who gets the kicks? Why, we do, and we can't retaliate. We can't squeal because we don't know anything. We're just like a lot of kids doing as we're told without knowing who issues the orders, and I don't like that, Steve. I'd like to know who I'm dealing with.'

Copping, who had had similar thoughts, nodded. 'So would I.'

'I'm not saying that this fellow ain't clever, or that we could do better ourselves. He's got an organizing brain that's put a lot of money in our pockets, and I'm not grumbling. But if he liked, he could shop the lot of us and there'd be no backwash, because we don't know 'im from Adam. See what I mean?'

Mr. Copping saw very clearly what he meant. He had merely expressed his own ideas on the subject of the unknown.

'I think,' continued Joe Hickman, 'we'll have to try and level things up a bit more.'

'How?'

'Well,' said the big man thoughtfully, 'what's to prevent you following 'im one night after you've finished at Gallows Wharf?'

'Not me, Joe,' broke in Mr. Copping emphatically. 'I'm pretty fond o' life, and I don't want to be taken out of the river one mornin' and shoved on a cold slab in the mortuary. If there's any followin' to do, you can do it yourself.'

'You needn't let him know you're following him.'

'You wouldn't have to let him know! He knows everything, that fellow. I believe he can read your thoughts. The same idea occurred to me some months ago and I decided to do it. The night I made up my mind to find out who he was, just before I left him, he turned to me and said, 'If you've ever any idea in your mind of findin' out who I am, you can forget it. The man who knows me 'ull wake up in hell!' '

'Must have been a coincidence,' grunted Mr. Hickman. 'You can't pull that thought-reading stuff over me, Steve. However, there's no reason why we should do it ourselves. Why not get Salty or little Ted Smith to do it. I'm telling you, Steve, we ought to know more about him for our own sakes. It 'ud be a safeguard in case anything happens. I don't say as anything is going to happen, but it might, and then where are we? In the soup!' He took the cigar out of his mouth and spat out some shreds of tobacco. 'Did you see this fellow Macintyre?' he asked abruptly.

Steve Copping nodded. 'Yes,' he began, and at that moment a soft whir came from a corner of the room.

Joe Hickman uttered an oath. 'That's the buzzer,' he said. 'The busies are here!'

Mr. Copping went a little pale. 'What can they want?' he muttered. 'Do you think — '

'I don't think anything!' snarled Joe Hickman. 'Most likely it's nothing. They often come snooping around.' He pressed a button twice on his desk. 'Sit tight and don't worry. They won't find nothing. There's a little poker game going on at the back of the 'all, but by the time they get to the room they'll only find a few fellows playin' dominoes, and there's no law agin that. Come in,' he said as somebody tapped at the door.

It opened and Sam appeared. 'This fellow wants to see you, Mr. Hickman,' he announced, and over his shoulder Joe Hickman saw the tall figure of Terry Ward.

6

Copping Is Alarmed

The young inspector came into the office and sniffed. 'Why don't you open your windows,' he said pleasantly, 'and let in a little fresh air? The atmosphere of this place is unbreathable.'

'You needn't breathe it if you don't like it, Mr. Ward,' growled Joe Hickman. 'Not that I'm not always pleased to see you. In fact I'm glad for the police to come to my premises at any time. Everything's open and above-board.'

'I'm sure you are, and I'm sure it is,' said Terry. 'You're a wonderful fellow, Joe. You're so straight that a foot-rule beside you would look crooked!'

'Honesty is the best policy,' said Mr. Hickman virtuously. 'I always say that.'

'You say such a lot of things that aren't true! You've got quite a respectable lot here tonight.'

'All the people that come here are respectable. Some of them are a bit wild, but there's no harm in 'em.'

'What about Lew Felan and Ginger Smith?' asked Terry sarcastically. 'They used to be clients of yours, and now they're serving long stretches for half killing the night watchman of a barge. What d'you call that? Just high spirits?'

'You can't help gettin' bad characters in occasionally,' protested Mr. Hickman. 'But if I know 'em, I won't let 'em pass the door. I've always tried to keep this place select.'

'There must be something wrong with your selector. It's no good trying that stuff on me; you ought to have better sense. You know as well as I do that this place harbours some of the worst characters in the neighbourhood.'

'Did you come here to tell me that?' said Mr. Hickman, his small eyes regarding the other venomously.

'No. I came here to see Steve Copping.'

'To see me?' exclaimed Mr. Copping in alarm. 'Why, Mr. Ward, what did you want to see me about?'

'How long have you been here?' asked Terry, and the other knit his brows.

'I can't rightly say,' he answered. 'How long have I been here, Joe?'

'Most of the evening,' grunted Mr. Hickman. 'We was just havin' a chow together, Mr. Ward.'

'You've been here most of the evening, eh?' said Terry. 'You haven't been up west?'

Mr. Copping's face was a picture of innocence as he shook his head. 'Up west, Mr. Ward? Whatever put that idea into your head?'

'You did!' said Terry Ward shortly. 'Stop lying, Copping! You were seen to enter and leave a block of flats in Swallow Street earlier this evening.'

'Well, supposing I was?' said Mr. Copping, and his eyes were alert and watchful. 'To tell you the truth, Mr. Ward, I *did* go up west. I didn't want to say so before because — well, I went to visit a lady friend of mine. You're a man of the world and you understand.'

'Miss Roy Macintyre, I presume?' said Terry, and Copping was taken aback.

'I don't know what you mean,' he mumbled. 'I don't know any Miss Macintyre.'

'I know you don't,' broke in the young inspector. 'But Roy Macintyre was the only friend you visited, and I want to know why.'

'I've never 'eard of any law that prevents a man visitin' his friends,' protested Mr. Copping, but the expression on his face was uneasy.

'There isn't, but it'll take a lot to make me believe that you're a friend of the managing director of a firm like Macintyre and Sloan.'

'Well, I'm not exactly a friend of his.' Copping was rapidly exercising his brain to think of some plausible explanation for his visit. 'Perhaps I might say a business acquaintance.'

'Perhaps you might say a lot of things!' snapped Terry Ward. 'But suppose you try telling the truth for a change.'

'I *am* tellin' you the truth, Mr. Ward,' said Copping in an injured voice. 'I wouldn't try and deceive the police. I've got too great a respect for 'em, particularly the river police.'

'A fine body of men! The best in the world!' declared Mr. Hickman, nodding his large head in agreement. 'You know me, Mr. Ward. I wouldn't have nothin' to do with a man what didn't do all he could to help the police in the execution of their duty.'

Terry's eyes twinkled, and he looked from one to the other admiringly. 'I must say you do it very well. It sounds almost genuine. Now let's have it, Copping. Why did you go to see Mr. Macintyre?'

'Well, as a matter of fact, it was about some private business. He wanted me to arrange — I don't know whether I ought to tell you this because 'e wanted it kept dark, but I know you can be trusted.'

'Thank you,' murmured Terry.

'He wanted me to arrange,' continued Mr. Copping, 'with a friend of mine in Belgium for a large consignment of bricks. There you are, now you know the truth, Mr. Ward. I 'ope you won't let it go no further. There's a rival firm who'd like to get in first — ' His imagination was working overtime that night. ' — so it's a secret, if you understand.'

'I see,' said Terry, who did nothing of the kind. 'And Macintyre approached you — bricks being your business, I suppose?'

'Well, not exactly.' Mr. Copping cleared his throat. 'He came to me because I knew these people in Belgium and could get them for him at a lower price.' He saw the disbelief in the inspector's eye and added hastily: 'That's the truth, Mr. Ward, if I never move from here.'

Terry looked at him steadily for a moment in silence. 'What's the name of the firm in Belgium with whom you are such good friends?' he inquired.

Mr. Copping was momentarily nonplussed. His friend, Joe Hickman, came to his rescue. 'You're not entitled to ask these questions, under the Act, Mr. Ward,' he protested. 'You know that as well as I do.'

'Since when have you taken up law, Joe?' said Terry, who was well aware that he spoke the truth. 'We shall have you blossoming forth one of these days into a lawyer, like Steve here, who has become a leading merchant in the City of London. Well, you needn't worry; I'm not going to ask any more questions except one,' he added abruptly. 'What rank do you two hold in the River Men?'

The abruptness of the question staggered his listeners. A look of consternation came into the large, flabby face of Mr. Hickman, and Steve Copping licked his suddenly dry lips. It was the big man who first recovered himself.

'You'll have your little joke, won't you, Mr. Ward?' he said smoothly, and the only sign of his emotion was that his voice was a little more husky than usual. 'What should we know about the River Men, a gang of thieves and murderers? We're respectable, hard-working people. We don't know nothing about such things.'

'I thought I'd just ask,' said Terry Ward pleasantly, and he was satisfied, for he had seen all he wanted to know in the faces of the two men. 'Let me give you a warning, Hickman. You've been lucky up to now; don't try your luck too far, as it may desert you. And if the cells at Pentonville are cleaner than this office, they're not nearly so comfortable. Good night!'

He turned on his heel with this parting shot and left the office, accompanied by the gaping Sam, who had been an agitated audience.

For some seconds after he had gone, Copping and Joe Hickman stared at each other in silence, and it was the former who spoke first.

'D'you think — d'you think he knows anything?' he asked hoarsely.

'If he did we shouldn't be sitting here now. No, he doesn't know anything. He'd have pulled us in if he did. But I believe he suspects. You must have been followed tonight, Steve.'

The other nodded slowly. 'Yes,' he said uneasily. 'I don't like the sound of it, Joe. It looks to me as though Ward was on to something. Do you think I'd better cancel this interview tonight?'

'No,' said Hickman after a pause. 'He wants to see you pretty urgently. Anyway, there's no means of letting him know now. I should go, but take extra precautions. Go to Gallows Wharf by a roundabout route and make sure you're not followed.' He took the bottle out of the cupboard and poured out two stiff drinks. Steve Copping seized his eagerly and gulped it down.

'I needed that,' he gasped, wiping his lips with the back of his hand. 'That fellow coming here like that gave me a pretty bad turn, I can tell you.'

Joe Hickman swallowed his whisky slowly, set down his empty glass, and pursed his lips. 'One of these days,' he said softly, 'Mr. Blooming Inspector Terrence Ward will be taken from the river with his head bashed in. And the day that happens, I'll stand free drinks to everybody in the place!'

7

The Interview

It was nearing half-past two, and a scud of grey-black cloud veiled the sky. The rain which had been falling earlier in the evening had waned to a fine drizzle, and Greenwich in the neighbourhood of the river looked even less inviting than it usually did. The narrow streets were deserted, their rain-swept surfaces glistening in the reflected light of the street lamps. The river itself, an oily mass of moving water with only a few riding lights of anchored vessels twinkling eerily in the darkness, was whipped occasionally to froth by the keen wind which had sprung up. The gaunt bulk of the warehouse on Gallows Wharf looked menacing as it reared its black silhouette against the only slightly lighter background of the sky.

With the exception of the night patrols moving leisurely over their various beats, there was no one abroad.

A clock somewhere on the Middlesex bank chimed the half-hour, and coincident with the sound, a man turned out of a narrow alley and went slouching along towards the river. He had to bend his head to resist the driving impulse of the rain, and the cloth cap he wore pulled down low over his eyes, together with his upturned collar, effectually concealed his face. He came out on the waterfront, and rounding a great pile of timber, glanced in the direction of the out-jutting building that constituted the warehouse on Gallows Wharf. It lay to his right, barely fifty yards away, but it was possible to reach it by negotiating a narrow strip of broken frontage. A flash of light sprang for a moment from the torch he carried in his left hand. The glimmer only lasted for a second, but it was sufficient to illuminate the sodden, broken woodwork of the wharf along which he had decided to make his way.

Stepping out from the shelter of the timber, he began cautiously to advance along the narrow footway. Once he almost lost his footing and fell into the swirling waters of the river, regaining it only with an effort and a muttered exclamation. It took him some time to reach his objective, but presently he stood beneath the towering wall of the deserted warehouse.

It was pitch dark here, and after a pause he began to feel his way along the brickwork. Presently his groping hands touched the outlines of a narrow doorway. The door itself was fastened, but again the torch glimmered for an instant, and then from the darkness came the faint snap as something broke. The rusty lock had given under the force of the jemmy which he returned to his overcoat pocket.

Even now it required all his strength to open the long-disused door, but he succeeded sufficiently to be able to squeeze himself through. Once across the threshold he hesitated, shutting the door behind him. The warehouse was deserted, he knew, at present, but if his calculations were correct it would not be deserted long.

Slowly he moved forward, avoiding the cluttered lumber which littered the floor. Presently he had to use the torch again, but took the precaution of pointing the ray towards the rotting boards so that the light should stand the least chance of being seen.

After a quick glance round the place, he saw what he was looking for: a long ladder leading upwards from the ground floor into the darkness above. The torch went out once more, and he began to feel his way gingerly towards the ladder, skirting a pile of broken packing-cases, which he had noted, without difficulty. He made no sound as he moved, for his feet were shod with rubber-soled shoes.

Reaching the foot of the ladder, he gripped it with one hand and paused again to listen: No sound disturbed the silence except the patter of the raindrops on the windows and the sighing of the wind. Stealthily he began to climb the ladder, rung by rung. The darkness was so intense that even now his eyes had got used to it, he could see very little. Instinct rather than sight warned him when his head came through the open trap and above the level of the upper floor. He felt for the edge and found it at shoulder height. Gripping the moulding with his hands, he drew himself up and crawled clear of the trap. His hand went to his pocket, where he had put the torch. He dared not move here without first seeing the lie of the ground. There might be holes in the flooring where the woodwork had rotted. One false step and he would pitch headlong to the lower floor, with the risk of a broken leg — or something worse.

The light wavered over the dirty rubbish-littered boards and focused on the square opening through which the grain chute projected out over the river.

It was as well he had taken the precaution of using his light, for the flooring was broken in many places and looked flimsy and insecure. He had to risk it bearing his weight, however, and went forward, advancing one foot cautiously and testing its solidity at every step before trusting his whole weight upon it.

At a point where he had noticed a larger hole than most of the others, he came to a halt, and stretching himself at full length, applied his eye to the aperture. He looked into a pit of blackness which he knew masked the ground floor of the warehouse.

He was in plenty of time. The man he was waiting to see would not come to the warehouse until three. For many weeks, he had watched his arrival and departure, and knew that he was punctual to the second.

Making himself as comfortable as possible, he settled down to his long vigil. There was no sound except the whistling of the wind through the broken walls of the old structure and the faint squeaking and scuttling of rats in the room below.

Again he heard the clock strike, three faint strokes, and before the last note had faded to silence there came the creak of a board and a faint footfall. The man he had been waiting for had entered the building.

His body tensed, and he peered eagerly through the crack in the board, straining his eyes to pierce the darkness.

There came the scrape of a match, and the blackness fled before the faint glimmer of a yellow flame. He was looking almost directly down on to a plain deal table, over which a dark figure was bending. It straightened up, and in the light of the candle which it had lighted, the watcher caught a glimpse of the lined yellow face and protruding chin. The old man shuffled out of his line of vision and returned with a chair.

Seating himself at the table, he took some papers from the breast pocket of his shabby coat and began to examine them carefully.

A quarter of an hour passed, and the man on the floor above shifted stealthily to ease his cramped limbs. The occupant of the room below had produced a pencil and was making some notes on the documents in front of him when the soft 'burr' of a buzzer came from somewhere in the shadows of the huge apartment. It was obviously a signal, for the old man got up, walked round in front of the table, and stooping, pulled back a bolt in the floor and began to raise an oblong-shaped trap.

The eavesdropper caught a glimpse of swiftly running water, and the harsh voice of the old man murmured something. Fastened to rings in the floor beside the trap was a rope ladder, and after receiving a reply to his question, the crouching figure dropped one end of the ladder through the trap.

After a moment's delay, the head and shoulders of another man appeared through the opening. He mounted carefully, scrambled over the edge, and waited while the old man pulled up the ladder and closed the trap.

'Good morning, Copping,' said the harsh voice. 'Did you see Macintyre?'

Steve Copping took out a handkerchief and wiped his perspiring face. 'Yes, guv'nor, I saw 'im, and I've fixed things.'

'Good!' The old man, who had taken his seat behind the table, chuckled throatily. 'You've done well, Copping. You've redeemed the mistake you made when you sent that man Pelton to me.'

'I'd no idea he was a busy,' grunted

Copping. 'He took me in completely.'

'He nearly took me in as well. If he'd been a little less impatient, he'd have succeeded. As it was, he gave himself away, and — well, he won't bother us anymore.'

His eyes went towards the trap, and Mr. Copping, following the direction of his glance, shivered. Somewhere below that swirling yellow water, in the thick slime of Thames mud, lay all that was left of the detective who had so nearly brought about their ruin.

'Yes, you've done very well,' went on the old man. 'We've got Macintyre — like that!' He stretched out his open gloved hand and slowly closed the fingers.

'I had a bit of a shock tonight, though, guv'nor,' said Copping. 'I was followed to Macintyre's flat.'

'You were followed? How do you know?' rasped the other quickly.

Mr. Copping explained.

'That's bad! Very bad,' muttered the old man. 'You're sure no one followed you here?'

'Yes, I'm sure of that. I was careful.'

'We shall all have to be careful. This Ward is a man of ability, and a danger. I think, at the first available opportunity, he had better be . . . eliminated.'

'I'll put Noakes on to him. Give him a shot of coke and he'd shoot up his own mother.'

The old man nodded. 'Yes, Noakes is a very good instrument. You must get Ward, Copping, and get him soon, and Miss Lee.'

'Why her?'

'Because I say so,' snarled the other, 'and that's sufficient. You oughtn't to find it difficult. Get her near the river on a dark night and the thing's done. You can take precautions to see that she hasn't a chance of swimming.'

Copping growled something which the listener failed to catch.

'When I want your advice I'll ask for it,' snapped the man at the table. 'Your job is to do as you're told. You understand that?'

'All right, guv'nor,' said Copping soothingly. 'I didn't mean no harm. I suppose you've got your own reasons, but it struck me as being a waste of time to go after this woman. There's nothin' in it.'

'There's more in it than you know. And don't be under any misunderstanding. When I give an order, I'm going to have it carried out, see? You've got to go after Ward and Miss Lee, and get them both. Is that clear?'

'That's clear.'

'And continue to play up Macintyre. Get him so involved that he won't stand a chance of backing out. Now, let's go into the other matters.'

He rustled the papers in front of him, and Copping bent over the table. Their voices dropped to a low murmur, and the man above could hear nothing that was said, but he had heard enough to render the risk of his morning's excursion profitable.

For half an hour, the two men talked and argued. At the expiration of that time, the old man handed to his companion a sheet of paper covered with pencilled notes and rose to his feet. 'Now you'd better be going,' he said. 'I don't want to be long, I've got other things to attend to when I leave here.'

Copping stuffed the paper into his pocket and waited while the other pulled up the trap and arranged the rope ladder.

'At the same time on Tuesday,' said the old man harshly as the other lowered his body through the aperture.

Copping nodded and disappeared from view. The ladder was pulled up and the trap closed.

For five minutes after he had gone, the old man stood by the table, intent in thought; then he blew out the candle and the man above heard him shuffling across the floor. His footsteps faded to silence, and once more there was nothing to be heard but the wind and the cracks and creaks of the old building.

The watcher rose swiftly and made his way carefully to the head of the ladder. Descending, he crossed the littered floor below and cautiously let himself out of the warehouse by the way he had come. The rain had ceased but the wind was still blowing strongly, and he had difficulty in fighting his way along the narrow edge of wharfage that would eventually lead him back to the deserted stretch of Thames Street.

The morning light was creeping up the eastern sky when a taxi turned into the street in which Mr. Roy Macintyre lived, and that gentleman got out of the vehicle, paid the driver, opened the main doors of the building with his key, and ascended by the lift to his flat. Letting himself in, he passed into the study, poured himself out a whisky and soda, and drank it quickly.

Five minutes later he was in bed and asleep, tired, but thoroughly satisfied with his night's work.

8

The Letter

Catherine Lee occupied a bed-sitting room in a small house in Evelyn Street. It was not a very salubrious neighbourhood, but it suited her purpose and had the advantage of being within walking distance of Macintyre and Sloan. The room was clean and cheap, and if the furniture was sparse, what there was of it was comfortable.

Leisurely eating her breakfast, which Mrs. Walters, her landlady, had just brought her, Catherine read for the second time the letter which had come by that morning's post. Judging from the frown which wrinkled her forehead, its contents were not particularly pleasing.

She folded it and put it beside her plate, turning her attention to the coffee and eggs which formed her meal. The frown still lingered, and her thoughts were obviously far away.

The little clock on the mantelpiece, which was one of her few personal possessions, chimed nine, and rising from the table, she began to put on her hat and coat, preparatory to setting off for the day's work.

Jimmy S was in the vestibule as she entered the offices of Macintyre and Sloan, and greeted her with his usual genial smile. 'Good morning, Miss Lee,' he said. 'The weather has changed for the better.'

She murmured a conventional reply and made her way up the stairs to her own little room.

The storm of wind and rain of the previous night had blown itself out, and the morning was warm and bright, almost a perfect spring morning. Taking off her out-of-door things, Catherine went over to the communicating door that led to Macintyre's office and turned the handle. Peeping in, she saw that the room was deserted, and coming back to her desk started to sort through the mail.

It was one of the rules of Macintyre and Sloan, instituted by old Robert, that all the letters came to her to be opened, and were then passed on to the head of the firm or the general manager.

There was a larger post than usual this morning, and sitting down, she began her task. Slitting open the envelopes, she withdrew the contents, glanced through them quickly, and separated them into two heaps, one for the attention of James Swann and one for the head of the firm. There were several envelopes marked 'Personal' addressed to Hugh Macintyre, and these she left untouched.

She was halfway through when she came to a typewritten envelope addressed to Macintyre bearing a Belgian stamp. The contents consisted of a long string of words that had no rhyme or reason. It began with the conventional 'Dear Sir' and went on: 'Happiness, grass, Park, Road. Lamp, singer, coal, brick. Ship, tree, bath, cup, misery, brick. Book, packet, box, picture, case, tyre, bush, brick. Receive, thanks, kitchen, dog, station, brick. Mud, house, shoe, brush, pin, floor, clock, price, apple. Meat, drink, blanket.'

The signature was undecipherable.

Although the letter had been posted in Belgium, the words were English. She looked at it, puzzled, but concluded that it was some kind of code. The word 'brick' occurred four times.

She wondered as she put it on Macintyre's heap what it was all about. It was unusual for Macintyre and Sloan to receive code letters; in fact, she couldn't remember anything of a similar nature since she had first become a member of the firm, and her curiosity was aroused.

She picked up the letter again, looked at it, and came to a decision. She had just finished opening the last of the mail when the buzzer went, and picking up the pile of letters for Macintyre's perusal, she tapped on the communicating door and entered his office.

He was sitting at his broad desk, and she thought he looked rather tired and worn. 'Good morning,' he said brusquely. 'Leave my letters and I'll ring for you again in a few minutes.'

She laid the little heap of correspondence in front of him and went back to her own office. In answer to her ring, a boy appeared, and to him she gave the letters which necessitated the attention of Jimmy S. The boy had only been gone a minute or so when there came a tap on the door, and in answer to her 'Come in,' a woman entered. She was young and expensively dressed. The subtle fragrance of an exotic perfume filled the room as she stood hesitantly on the threshold.

'Is this Mr. Macintyre's office?' The surprise which Catherine had experienced at sight of this unusual visitor was deepened when she heard her speak. The voice was high and shrill with an underlying note of commonness, and now as she came further into the office and the sunlight that streamed through the window fell on her, Catherine saw that she was not as young as she had at first believed. The sunlight revealed lines beneath the cleverly applied makeup, and the wisp of golden hair that was visible beneath the small hat was patently unnatural.

'This is Mr. Macintyre's office,' answered Catherine. 'Do you wish to see him?'

'Yes. Will you tell him it's Mrs. Renfrew? Tell him that I met him in

America; he'll remember me.'

One of the things which had been puzzling Catherine since her arrival was made clear. The peculiar intonation was due to the slight traces of an American accent.

'If you'll wait just a moment,' she said, 'I'll tell Mr. Macintyre.' Going over to the inner office, she tapped, opened the door, and went in.

Roy Macintyre was glowering at the mysterious letter which he had spread out on the blotting-pad in front of him. He looked up with a frown as she entered. 'What do you want?' he asked harshly. 'I said I'd ring — '

'There's a lady to see you,' interrupted Catherine. 'A Mrs. Renfrew. She says she knew you in America.'

A startled look came into his eyes, and beneath the tan his face paled. 'Mrs. Renfrew?' he muttered. 'What the devil's she doing in England? All right, I guess you can send her in.'

Catherine came back to find the woman openly reading the papers on her desk. 'Will you go in to Mr. Macintyre?'

she said, and the visitor smiled sweetly.

'Thank you so much,' she replied, and crossed to the communicating door.

As she disappeared from sight, leaving a trail of perfume behind her, Catherine opened the window. She hated perfume in large quantities, and this woman had drenched herself in scent. It was a little surprising that Macintyre should be on friendly terms with such a person, and then she remembered the expression on his face when she had mentioned the name of the visitor, and concluded that the terms were not so friendly after all. Obviously the two had met in America; no doubt the visitor had recently arrived in England and had taken the opportunity to look up an old acquaintance.

Catherine sat down at her desk and prepared to continue with her morning's work, but her mind was still occupied with conjectures concerning the exotic creature who was at that moment closeted with the head of the firm. Had she been able to see or hear the interview that was taking place, she would have received something of a shock. Macintyre rose to greet his visitor with anything but a friendly expression on his dark saturnine face.

'Well, what do you want?' he demanded. 'How long have you been in England?'

'I came over last week,' said the woman, looking round the comfortable but shabby office. 'You haven't got much of a place here, have you?' she remarked disparagingly.

'Did you come all the way from America to see what my office was like?' he demanded sarcastically.

She smiled sweetly as she shook her head. 'Of course I didn't. I came to see you.'

He grunted and pulled out a cigarette case.

'You're not very polite,' she remarked with a pout. 'You might ask me to sit down.'

'You don't need me to ask you,' he said. 'There's a chair if you want to sit down.'

She sank gracefully into the chair by the side of the desk.

'I do think,' she said, 'you might have

given me a better welcome after I'd taken the trouble to come all the way to this outlandish place to see you.'

'I'm sorry,' he retorted sarcastically. 'If I'd known you had been coming, we'd have put the flags out and hired a band!'

She shrugged one shoulder. 'You always were a brute, Micky,' she said. 'You've really no manners at all. You don't know how to treat a lady.'

'I do when I meet one,' he answered. 'See here, Marion, what's the game? Just why have you taken the trouble to seek me out?'

'Surely your intelligence will tell you that,' she replied, looking up at him through half-closed eyes. 'You've struck a good graft, Micky.'

He looked at her, his thin lips set, and nodded slowly.

'I see,' he said. 'And you want your share. Is that it?'

'Naturally,' she murmured.

'Well, you'll get nothing!' He flung his freshly lighted cigarette into the fireplace. 'Nothing! You understand?'

Marion's face hardened, and she

discarded all pretence of friendliness. 'Is that so? We'll see about that. Perhaps you'd like me to go to your police headquarters and have a word with the Chief? I might be able to tell them something that'd interest them.'

'Blackmail, eh?' he said softly.

'You can call it what you like, but I'm coming in on this deal. It's a long time since you left America, and it's taken me a long time to trace you. But now that I've found you, I'm going to make that time profitable.'

There was a long silence, broken at length by Macintyre. 'Listen, Marion,' he said, and his tone was more conciliatory, 'there's no need for us to quarrel. You may be able to help me. Is Jack with you?'

'Now you're being like your old self,' said the Marion with a smile. 'Yes, Jack's with me. We're staying at the Chatterton Hotel in Berkley Street.'

'You may be able to help me,' muttered Macintyre, taking out his case and helping himself to another cigarette with a hand that was not quite steady. 'Why didn't Jack come with you?'

'He thought it was better if I conducted this preliminary interview on my own. Why not come up and have a little dinner with us and talk things over?'

'Are you free tonight?' he asked, and she nodded. 'Very well, then. I'll be at the Chatterton at eight. You'd better go now; I've got a lot of work to do.'

She rose without protest and walked to the door. 'You won't forget to come,' she said, pausing on the threshold, and there was a menace behind the simple words.

'No, no, I won't forget!' he said impatiently. 'I'll be there at eight.'

'Goodbye, then,' she said, and there was a smile on her face as she passed through Catherine's little room and made her way down the stairs to the vestibule.

For some minutes after she had gone, Macintyre stood frowning and biting his nails. Then, seating himself at his desk, he picked up the telephone and gave a number. There was some delay before he was connected, and his conversation with the man at the other end of the wire was brief.

The frown had cleared from his face

when he hung up the receiver, for he had reached his decision. Marion Renfrew was an unforeseen danger that threatened life and liberty, and that danger had to be eliminated.

He turned to the work which awaited him on his desk with a feeling of relief, for the first step towards that elimination had been taken.

9

A Near Thing

The police launch came slowly upstream, its lights reflected blearily in the black water. Earlier there had been a moon, but now the river was shrouded in almost complete darkness. A few lights dotted the bank, and here and there the riding light of an anchored vessel, but they did little more than accentuate the gloom.

Standing in the bows, Terry Ward looked keenly ahead. His visit to Joe Hickman on the night of Copping's return from his interview with Macintyre had been the result of a carefully thought-out plan. The detective, who was watching Macintyre's movements, reported Copping's visit to Scotland Yard, and this had been relayed to Terry at Wapping Station. He knew from experience that the easiest way to catch a crook was to get him on the run, and his visit to Hickman's had been for no other purpose. If he could scare these men, he might force them to do something which would give away their connection with the River Men, and possibly lead to the roundup of that criminal organization.

Many weeks of careful inquiry had resulted in convincing Terry Ward of one thing, and that was that the billiards saloon on the riverfront was closely mixed up with, if not the actual headquarters of, the gang whose depredations had caused something of a panic among the owners of warehouses and shipping. Not that he believed for one moment that either Joe Hickman or Steve Copping was the controlling brain. He knew them both pretty intimately, and could not bring himself to reconcile the organizing genius which showed behind the activities of the River Men with their capabilities.

He more than suspected Macintyre of being this unknown person, and the report of the Scotland Yard detective had strengthened his suspicion. Later that evening, after Copping had left, Macintyre had come out of his flat, dressed shabbily, and set off briskly in the direction of Piccadilly Circus. The trailer had followed him and had succeeded in keeping him in sight as far as the Strand. Here, Macintyre had either become aware that he was being shadowed or else had taken precautions to avoid any possibility of his movements being followed, for the man had lost him in one of the side-streets that lead down to the Embankment.

Having lost his man, he had done a very sensible thing. He had made his way back to Waverly Mansions and taken up his position at a point where he could watch the entrance, and just before dawn had seen Macintyre return in a taxi. The man had been away for the greater part of the night, and respectable heads of respectable businesses do not usually stay out all night.

Macintyre's mysterious movements, coupled with the discovery of his notecase under the dead body of the watchman, was sufficient evidence to Terry Ward to connect him with the series of robberies and murders for which the River Men had been responsible. But although it was sufficient evidence for him, it was far from sufficient for a jury. There was nothing to prevent Macintyre offering a reasonable explanation for his midnight excursion, and the police were chary of bringing a charge against anyone, particularly a leading businessman, unless they were pretty certain that it could be substantiated. It was Terry's hope that a close watch on Macintyre would result in the obtaining of the evidence he wanted — concrete evidence that a clever counsel would find difficult to upset.

The police launch nosed its way slowly past the ugly stretch that marked North Woolwich, and came into Woolwich Reach. The young inspector glanced towards the back of Hickman's Billiards Saloon as they went by, but the place was in complete darkness and there was no sight or sound of life. They kept as much as possible to midstream, keeping a sharp lookout for any suspicious circumstance, for the greatest mystery attaching to the River Men was that they had never been seen at their nefarious work. Robbery after robbery had been committed, but without the alert patrols catching so much as a glimpse of the perpetrators. This was the most puzzling aspect of their activities. This, and the method by which they succeeded in getting the stolen stuff away.

Terry had given much thought to these problems without arriving at any satisfactory solution. It seemed impossible, with the river constantly patrolled as it was by men on the lookout for the marauders, that they should be able to carry out their schemes with complete immunity from detection. Earlier that night, acting on information received, he had searched a couple of barges moored in a portion of the river below Wapping, but the information had proved inaccurate and nothing at all suspicious was found. The little Nose who had seen the barges being furtively loaded with cases, and had notified Terry at the Wapping Police Station, had made a mistake, for the cases, on inspection, contained nothing more serious than a consignment of brummagem goods that was being moved from one warehouse to another further up the river.

Near the Royal Naval College, they

passed another police launch going in the opposite direction, and acknowledged the hail of the steersman. 'Pretty cold for this time of the year,' grunted the sergeant at the wheel, and Terry nodded.

'The wind's shifted to the east,' he answered. 'Still, it's dry. That's the main thing.'

The deserted bulk of Gallows Wharf loomed up on their right, and Terry scarcely even glanced at the rotting structure, never dreaming that in that dilapidated building the intrepid Pelton had paid the penalty for his temerity, or that it held the secret of the River Men.

The launch continued on its way, the ripples from its wake gently rocking the moored vessels on either side. They passed the wharf belonging to Macintyre and Sloan and went on towards the Pool.

So far, the night had yielded nothing in the way of excitement; and then, suddenly, Terry stiffened and leaned forward over the bows.

'What is it?' asked Sergeant Porter.

'I thought I heard a splash somewhere ahead,' muttered the young inspector.

'Did you hear it?'

But the sergeant had heard nothing. At the particular moment when the sound had reached Terry's ears, he had been bending down fumbling in the locker beside the steering wheel.

Straining his eyes to pierce the darkness, Terry searched the black expanse of the river. The sound had been faint, a long distance ahead. At first he could see nothing, and then suddenly his hand clenched on the gunwale.

'Steer to port!' he cried sharply.

'What is it?' asked the sergeant.

'Something floating there!' snapped Terry. 'Near those barges by the Surrey shore!'

The launch veered and drew closer to the bank.

'There it is! Now you can see it more plainly. It looks like a body!'

'Some poor devil tired of life, I suppose,' grunted the sergeant, as under Terry's direction he skilfully brought the launch nearer to the floating object.

It disappeared as they reached it, sinking beneath the surface of the water, and then came up again. Terry leaned over the side and made a grab at the pathetic thing. His fingers closed on sodden clothing.

'Good God, it's a woman!' he exclaimed. 'Give me a hand, Porter.'

The sergeant shut off his engine and came to his assistance. Between them, they lifted the limp figure over the gunwale of the boat and laid it on the bottom. And then it was that Terry saw the face in the faint glimmer of the green light that illuminated the dashboard.

'My God!' he breathed, and his face went white, for he was staring at Catherine Lee!

'Is she dead?' asked the sergeant; and Terry, his throat suddenly dry, bent down and searched for the heart. A great flood of relief swept over him when he felt a faint pulsing beneath his hand.

'No, she isn't dead!' he cried. 'Her heart's still beating. Make for the nearest police float, Sergeant, and get a move on. We must get a doctor to her at once!'

The sergeant sprang to his controls, and the powerful little engine chugged to life. The launch swept forward at full speed as Terry, taking off his coat, rolled it up and made an improvised pillow for Catherine's head.

Her eyes were closed and she was quite unconscious. On the whiteness of her forehead was a blue swelling, and Terry's brows drew together as he noticed it. Either she had struck her head after entering the water, or someone had given her a blow to ensure she was unable to swim. Terry thought the latter was the most likely. Catherine did not strike him as the type to attempt suicide, which left only two alternatives — an accident or attempted murder.

In an agony of impatience, he did what he could to make her comfortable while the launch sped on its way to the police float. It seemed an age, but in reality it was less than five minutes since they had taken her out of the water before the launch drew into the river station and was made fast by the willing hands of a river policeman. A stretcher was brought, and Catherine was lifted gently out and carried into the low-roofed building. In an incredibly short space of time a doctor arrived, and after a hasty examination

117

pronounced his verdict.

'She'll live,' he said shortly. 'But the shock has been a severe one. We'd better rush her to hospital and get these wet things off.'

A policeman was sent for a wheeled hand ambulance, and Catherine, who was still unconscious, was lifted onto this and hurried away to the nearest hospital, the doctor having already made arrangements for her reception on the telephone.

'How did she come to get in the water?' asked the inspector in charge of the river station.

'I don't know,' Terry replied grimly, 'but I've a suspicion somebody threw her in because they thought she knew something that was dangerous to their safety.'

That was as far as he put his thoughts into words. What was really at the back of his mind was the fact that Catherine Lee was a member of the staff of Macintyre and Sloan. Had she accidentally discovered something concerning Roy Hugh Macintyre that made her removal essential; something which connected him indisputably with the murderous activities of the River

Men? Perhaps when she recovered consciousness, she would be able to offer valuable information.

But in this he was to be disappointed, for Catherine Lee could tell him very little concerning the midnight adventure in which she had so nearly lost her life.

10

Catherine's Story

It was ten o'clock on the following morning when Terry arrived at the hospital to which Catherine had been taken, and was shown into the ward where she lay, propped up with pillows. Except for the paleness of her face and the dark bruise on her forehead, she looked little the worse for her experience, and greeted him with a smile that set his pulse racing.

'Good morning,' she said. 'Is this an official or a friendly visit?'

'Both,' he answered, standing at the foot of the narrow bed, surveying her critically. 'How are you feeling?'

'Fine. I wanted to get up but they wouldn't let me.'

'Quite right, too. I suppose you know that you ought to be thankful you're alive?'

'Yes,' she said, in a low voice. 'I'm terribly grateful, Mr. Ward.'

'It was the nearest thing I ever want to see,' he said fervently. 'Now tell me — how did you come to get in the water?'

She looked at him, and he received the impression that she was reluctant to speak about her adventure.

'I — I don't know,' she said hesitantly.

He raised his eyebrows. 'You must have some idea,' he suggested. 'Was it an accident?'

She shook her head slowly. 'No, it wasn't an accident. What I meant when I said I didn't know was that it was all so confused that it's very difficult to remember.'

She paused, and he waited patiently.

'I was down on Balkans Wharf,' she went on at length, 'when a man came out of the shadows of a pile of packing cases and attacked me, and that's all I remember.'

He stared at her in amazement. 'What on earth were you doing on Balkans Wharf at that time of night?'

'I — I . . . ' She hesitated. 'I couldn't

sleep. I had a bad headache. I thought perhaps a walk in the fresh air would do me good. I'm rather fond of the river by night.' She made no mention of the letter she had received the previous morning, which had been the real reason for her presence on Balkans Wharf at so late an hour.

'I see,' said Terry gravely. 'You were just out for a walk.'

'Yes.' She nodded, but there was a tinge of red in her pale cheeks. She found it very difficult to lie convincingly to this steady-eyed man, and lying she was.

'I see,' he said again. 'And this man who attacked you — can you give any description of him?'

'No, I never had a chance to see him.'

He saw her embarrassment, guessed that she was keeping something back and was puzzled. What did she have to hide? Not for a moment did he believe her explanation as to why she had been near the river at that hour of the night. He was too used to the expressions on people's faces when they were lying not to know whether he was being told the truth or not, and this woman was not telling the truth. There was a mystery here which he could not fathom. Of all people in the world, he would have imagined Catherine Lee to be the most honest, and yet, here she was, behaving like one of the crooks who were so constantly passing through his hands.

'They'll wonder at Macintyre and Sloan's what's happened to me,' she said, breaking the awkward silence. 'I should have been there an hour ago.'

'Don't worry about that, Miss Lee. If you like, I'll notify them of what's happened.'

'I wish you would,' she said gratefully. He chatted to her for a few moments longer, and then took his leave, greatly puzzled and more than a little worried. What was the reason for this mysterious attack on her, an attack that had very nearly been the means of ending her life? And why was she so reluctant to tell all she knew about it? Was she shielding someone, and was this someone Roy Macintyre?

Terry Ward was not without knowledge

of the romantic nature of young women, and it was quite conceivable that Catherine Lee might have contracted an infatuation for the dark and saturnine Macintyre. He was of a type likely to appeal to women of all ages, and particularly to young, un-sophisticated ones like Catherine. Yet surely, if he had been responsible for the attack, she would not be foolish enough to conceal the fact.

He reached Butcher Road and the entrance to Macintyre and Sloan's without having arrived at a solution to his problem. Jimmy S was chatting to the timekeeper in the vestibule and greeted him with a smile.

'Another police visit?' he said. 'What's the matter this time?'

'I'm not here officially,' said Terry. 'I have a message from Miss Lee.'

The smile left Swann's face and he became grave. 'What's happened to her?' he asked quickly. 'I've just been asking Brown here whether any message had been received from her.'

Terry explained briefly, and the general manager showed his concern. 'Good gracious, how dreadful!' he exclaimed. 'Who could have been responsible for such an outrage?'

'That's what I'd like to find out. Apparently Miss Lee was taken too much by surprise to see anything of her attacker.'

Jimmy S shook his head. 'It's a nasty neighbourhood,' he remarked. 'A dangerous neighbourhood. All sorts of undesirables congregate by the river and in the side-streets at night.'

'You're telling me.'

'I suppose it *is* rather like bringing coals to Newcastle,' said Swann with a wry smile. 'How is Miss Lee? I hope her condition isn't serious?'

'No, she's almost recovered now. In fact, she told me to tell you that she'd be in as usual tomorrow.'

'I'd better let Mr. Macintyre know. It's very kind of you, Inspector, to have troubled to come round.'

'It was no trouble,' said Terry. 'I was passing this way anyway.'

He took his leave, and for the first time as he turned in the direction of Creek Road realized how tired he was. He had had no sleep at all on the previous night, and that, coupled with his anxiety concerning Catherine, had left him spent. He was off duty until six o'clock that evening, and he decided to go home and have a rest.

He lived in a small house in one of the better-class streets in Stepney. It was not exactly a salubrious neighbourhood, but it suited him, and was within easy distance of the river police Station at Wapping.

A bus carried him to the top of the street, and he let himself in with his key. Mrs. Keston, the motherly woman who looked after his needs and acted as housekeeper, met him in the hall.

'You're late, Mr. Ward,' she said with a smile. 'I had your breakfast ready an hour and a half ago. I'm afraid it's spoiled now.'

'Don't worry,' said Terry, as he took off his hat and coat. 'I don't want anything. I'll just have a cup of tea and go to bed.'

'You look tired,' she said sympathetically, and as she was turning away: 'Oh, I've just remembered. There was a man here early this morning from Scotland Yard.'

'Scotland Yard?' said Terry in surprise.

'That's what he said, sir. He had an important message for you, and he waited for a little while, but he couldn't wait no longer, so he left a note. You'll find it in the sitting-room, sir.'

Wondering what the urgent message could be about, Terry opened the door of the cosy little apartment and entered. He saw the note propped up against the clock on the mantelpiece, and going over carried it to his writing-table.

It was one of his peculiarities that he invariably opened all letters by slitting the top of the envelope with a paper-knife, and this habit undoubtedly saved his life. He felt the edge of the knife grate against something as he slipped it under the flap, and a moment or two later discovered the reason. Along the inside of the envelope, just under the fold of the flap, had been pasted a narrow strip of tape, and in this were embedded a dozen or more needle points, each one covered with a gummy substance that shone greenly in the light from the window. Had he adopted the usual method of opening the envelope by sliding his thumb under the flap, nothing could have prevented one or more of the venomous little spikes from piercing his flesh.

'Very pretty!' he murmured through clenched teeth. 'Very pretty indeed! Now who was the genius, I wonder, responsible for thinking of this?'

11

The Robbery at Moxon's

The night watchman at Moxon's, the ivory importers, laid aside the evening newspaper he had been reading, yawned, and glanced at the clock on the wall of his little office. It was half-past one, time for his second round. Picking up the revolver that lay near his hand, he twirled the cylinder, reassured himself that it was loaded by a glance at the shining ends of the cartridges, although he needed no such assurance, and slipping the weapon into his pocket, rose to his feet.

Carefully and conscientiously he made a tour of the big warehouse, found everything in order, and came back to his room to heat the coffee which he was in the habit of drinking at this period of the night. Smoking was strictly prohibited by the rules of the firm, but Mr. Wicker was not a close adherent to rules and regulations.

'A whiff or two don't do a man no harm,' he had explained often to his wife. 'It 'elps to pass the time and soothes the nerves. And blimey, Annie, you can take it from me that yer need somethin' to soothe 'em with the funny noises what goes on in a place like ours at night. If mine weren't pretty steady, I'd 'ave got the creeps at my job long ago.' There was some truth in this statement, for the sounds in the big building at times were peculiar and varied.

Mr. Wicker carefully put a match to a small gas ring and placed upon it a can of lukewarm coffee. While this was heating, he took from his waistcoat pocket a short black clay pipe, and produced from a small tin a length of ship's plug, cut off a piece and rubbed it gently between his palms. Replacing the jack-knife he had used and the tobacco back in his pocket, he methodically filled the bowl of his pipe, lit it, and began to puff with evident enjoyment.

The silence around him was profound. The creaks and cracks, and the odd little scurryings that sometimes disturbed his peace, were absent tonight. Most likely it was because there was no wind. He had noticed before that they were more pronounced when it was high.

The liquid in the can began to bubble, and taking a cup from the shelf beside his stool, Mr. Wicker lifted the can off the gas ring by its wire handle, splashed some of the thick black liquid into the cup, added sugar and milk, and gulped some of the scalding mixture noisily.

'That's better,' he said aloud, and turned to put out the gas ring.

'If you make a sound you'll die!' hissed a voice, and the pipe fell from Mr. Wicker's lips and smashed to pieces on the concrete floor. 'Put your hands up!' went on the hoarse whisper. 'If you try to reach that pistol in your pocket, it'll be the last movement you'll make!'

The watchman swung round with a dropped jaw. In the open doorway of his small office stood a weird figure clad from head to foot in black, and holding in one gloved hand a wicked-looking automatic.

'Here — who the hell — ' began Mr. Wicker.

'Keep quiet!' broke in the man in the doorway. 'If you don't give any trouble, you'll be unharmed; but if you make a fuss — well, I've told you what'll happen.'

Mr. Wicker blinked painfully. Beyond the man who was covering him he could see dim black-clad shapes flitting about noiselessly, and into his dull brain seeped the explanation of this phenomenon.

'Blimey! The River Men!' he gasped.

A second figure, black-clad and masked like the man with the gun, squeezed into the room. A cloth drenched with the pungent fumes of chloroform was whipped over Mr. Wicker's head, and from thence until he recovered consciousness some hours later, the subsequent proceedings interested him not at all.

The man who had administered the drug looked at the motionless form of the watchman and nodded in satisfaction. 'He won't trouble us for some time,' he muttered.

The other man grunted approvingly. 'You'd better stop here and keep an eye on him. I'll tell the others to get busy.'

He moved away, making no noise in his

rubber shoes, and joined half a dozen men who were waiting in the dark vestibule.

'O.K.,' he said. 'Jump to it! Get the vault open.'

Unlike the majority of warehouses, Moxon's possessed an unusual feature. Dealing as they did in the valuable commodity of ivory, it was necessary to have a safe storage for this precious substance, and a vault built of reinforced concrete had been added to the original building, entered by means of a large steel door.

Four of the marauders made their way swiftly to the stairs leading down to the vault, carrying with them the apparatus they had brought for the purpose of forcing the door. There was no fuss, no hurry. Every movement was carried out smoothly and without haste. But there was one thing they had not reckoned with.

Mr. Ernest Moxon, the managing director of the firm, had read a great deal concerning the activities of the River Men, and had spent much time in thinking out how he could best safeguard his property from the possible depredations of the thieves. And he had hit upon a plan which he had kept secret, even from the staff.

A large cargo of ivory had arrived three days previously, and aware that this might attract the attention of the river robbers, he had entered into a conspiracy with his night watchman and the police. It was the duty of Mr. Wicker, besides making his usual hourly inspection of the building, to ring up the local police station every hour throughout the night to say that all was well.

Sergeant Yarrow, sitting in the quiet charge-room at Old Water Lane Station, looked over his spectacles at the slow-ticking wall clock and frowned. The message from Moxon's was five minutes overdue. Had old Wicker fallen asleep, or was there a more serious explanation? He decided to wait another five minutes before taking any action, and helped himself from the jug of coffee which the night orderly had just brought in.

The hands of the clock moved slowly

on, but the telephone remained silent. Still frowning, the grey-haired sergeant got laboriously down from his stool, crossed the charge-room and tapped on the door of his superintendent's office.

Superintendent North looked up from his littered desk as the sergeant's head came round the door.

'There's been nothing through from Moxon's, sir,' announced Yarrow.

'Nothing through?' said the superintendent. 'When did you receive the last message?'

'Over an hour and ten minutes ago.'

North pursed his lips. 'Wonder if the watchman's fallen asleep,' he muttered.

'I thought that, sir. That's why I waited for ten minutes. What shall I do? Give him a ring?'

North considered for a second, and then shook his head. 'No, don't do that. If there's anything wrong, we shall scare our birds away. All right, Sergeant, I'll deal with this.'

He picked up his telephone, and a second later was talking to the night officer in charge at Scotland Yard. The night man jotted down his information on a pad at his elbow, rang for a messenger, tore off the sheet and sent it up to the information room.

The information room at Scotland Yard was the nerve centre of that big building. Here, as you entered, were four glass-covered tables bearing maps and brass pegs which, at a glance, gave the location of every wireless car throughout the metropolitan area. There were round pegs to indicate the patrol cars and square pegs to show the position of the 'Q' cars. The famous Flying Squad were allowed to go anywhere in London, and they were not shown on this map. It was divided into the four operating districts, each of which was in the charge of a chief constable and was split into many sections, each lettered and numbered. Wireless and other cars operating in these sections were given the corresponding numbers which were sent out on the messages broadcast to all cars from this room. But the only cars who answered the call were those bearing the particular number allotted to the district where their assistance was required.

The sub-divisional inspector in charge received the message relayed by Superintendent North, glanced at the map, and two seconds later the wireless operator was tapping out instructions in code to all cars bearing the particular number that covered the district occupied by Moxon's. Within twenty minutes of Superintendent North's telephone message being received, six police cars laden with armed men were converging from all points on the warehouse by the river. One of these cars stopped at the police station to pick up North.

'I don't know whether there's anything doing,' said the superintendent to the officer in charge. 'Maybe we shall find the watchman asleep. I'm merely carrying out instructions.'

'If there *is* anything doing,' said the sergeant in control of the squad car, 'it'll be the first time these birds have been surprised.'

They reached the neighbourhood of the warehouse to discover the other five cars already waiting. There was a hurried conference, and men were stationed so that the building was surrounded on three sides. The headquarters of the Thames Police at Wapping had been notified by telephone, and two fast launches were hurrying to take charge of the river frontage.

Moxon's was dark and silent. There was no sound from within or without. Superintendent North, accompanied by one of the squad men, made a cautious inspection of the outside of the premises, but there was nothing to show that anything unlawful was taking place. No vehicle had been found parked in any of the numerous side-streets, and if the River Men were at work, it looked as if they must have come by water.

A winking light from the direction of the river told the land men that the river police had arrived. All forms of exit from the premises were now cut off. North consulted with the officer in charge of the mobile force.

'We'll take half a dozen of your men and effect an entrance,' he said. 'That ought to bolt our quarry if there's anyone there.'

The mobile man agreed.

Six armed men, led by North, scaled the big gates that gave admittance to the yard of the warehouse and crossed cautiously to the main doors. They were within two yards of them when they were suddenly flung open, and from the darkness within came a fusillade of shots. One of the men with North dropped, groaning, with a bullet through his shoulder.

The police fired an answering volley and made a rush for the entrance. As they did so, half a dozen black-clad shapes came pouring down the shallow steps, the pistols they held spitting fire and death. Another of the detectives crumpled up, shot dead in his tracks, and then it became a hand-to-hand struggle. Reinforcements, attracted by the shooting, climbed the big gates and came to North's assistance.

In a very short time it was all over and the river robbers were under arrest.

'That was hot while it lasted,' panted North, wiping the blood from his face where a bullet had chipped the cheekbone. 'We'll get these birds along to the cooler and examine our catch later.'

12

The Man Who Knew

Two of the river thieves had been seriously wounded, and these, together with the wounded detective and the dead officer, were taken away on an ambulance that had been hurriedly sent for. Three others had attempted escape by the river, and these had fallen into the hands of the river police, in charge of Terry, who greeted Superintendent North with a grin.

'Quite a profitable night's work,' he said, and the land man agreed.

The bag consisted of seven of the River Men, typical river rats for the most part, with the exception of two, who seemed a little more superior than their fellows. Terry discovered a long black-painted launch moored to the river frontage of Moxon's, and it was by this, he concluded, the men had come. A search of the warehouse

140

revealed the unfortunate watchman, who was beginning to recover consciousness. The robbers had been disturbed none too soon. The steel door of the vault had already been opened, the lock having been cut out with a powerful oxyacetylene blow-pipe, and already some of the ivory had been taken out and piled in the vestibule.

'How they were going to get this away beats me,' said Terry as he and Superintendent North stood looking at the bulky substance. 'They couldn't have got a tenth of this in the launch, that's certain.'

'How did they get any of the other stuff away?' said the superintendent. He was beginning to feel the reaction, and his cheek was paining him considerably. 'Well, we've got seven of them, anyway.'

Terry nodded. 'Perhaps they'll be able to tell us something that will lead us to the rest. And particularly to the fellow in control of them. He's the man I want.'

By the time they had finished their inspection of the vault and the rest of the warehouse, the night watchman had sufficiently recovered to be able to tell his story. It was not very helpful. The means

141

by which the thieves had gained entrance was ingenious. The crane used to hoist the goods to the various floors of the warehouse hung ten feet from the ground, by the barred doors of the platform. The ledge of this platform projected a foot, and beside it was a narrow window which the watchman informed them was left open for ventilation purposes, as it was considered to be out of reach of any unauthorized intruder. The crane chain ended in a weighted ball below which was a hook, and the thieves, with the aid of a light pole, had passed a rope through this hook, pulled it double, and one of their number had swarmed up to the ledge and crawled through the open window, admitting the rest by means of a side door.

Terry succeeded in obtaining this information from a little wizened-faced man whom he recognized at once. 'What else do you know, Weedy?' he asked.

The little man shook his head. 'I don' know nothin'. You've got me an' it's a fair cop.'

'You'll get ten years for this, Smith,' said Superintendent North, to whom

Weedy Smith was no stranger. 'Carrying firearms is a serious offence, and you know it.' Beneath the grime on his face, the river rat went pale.

'We might be lenient with him,' said Terry, winking at the superintendent, 'if he'd spill the beans. Who's the fellow behind you, Weedy? Who issues the orders?'

But here Mr. Smith could offer no information, and Terry was inclined to believe his protestations when he assured them that he knew nothing. The man was in such a panic that if he had been in possession of any information, he would have been only too pleased to part with it.

Mr. Moxon, a thin cadaverous man who had been notified of the assault on his property, arrived in a car just as dawn was breaking. He took the entire credit for the capture of the thieves to himself, and to a certain extent he was right. But for the arrangement he had made with North and the watchman, the robbery would probably have gone undiscovered until the arrival of the staff in the morning. The prisoners were taken to the station and closely questioned, but they maintained a stolid silence, and either could not or would not supply any information concerning the organization to which they belonged.

Terry Ward thought they one and all looked scared, and in this he was right, for the man who had brought them into being was a dangerous master to serve; and even had they known anything, fear of the consequences would have kept them from squealing.

* * *

The evening editions of the newspapers carried a long account of the affair, and a certain Mr. Swinger, occupying an unpretentious back bedroom in Watergate Lane, Greenwich, read the story with interest. He was a pale man with thin mouse-coloured hair and an expression of permanent discontent. His worldly possessions consisted of thirty shillings, the remnants of his carefully hoarded savings. But this fact worried him very little, for Mr. Swinger possessed knowledge that he was certain would provide him with a comfortable competence for the rest of his life.

He read the account in the newspaper twice, and turned to the thick slabs of bread and butter and weak tea which his landlady had provided for his frugal supper. Yes, there was money in plenty waiting to be picked up, waiting to be had for the asking. Mr. Swinger's thin mouth curled upwards slightly at the corners, the nearest approach it had ever got to a smile. He should receive an answer to his letter at any time now, and that the answer would be favourable he never doubted. Even while his thoughts were concentrated on the subject, he heard the muffled rat-tat of the postman, followed presently by the heavy tread of his landlady as she ascended the stairs. She tapped and entered, carrying a letter in her hand which she laid on the table at his side.

'For you, Mr. Swinger,' she said unnecessarily, and added: 'I 'ope it's good news. I don't charge much for the room, but I likes it reg'lar, and I've got things of me own to meet.'

'I will settle up your account at the end of the week, Mrs. Rose,' said Mr. Swinger with dignity.

'I 'ope you will, sir,' she said meaningfully, and went out.

Mr. Swinger looked at the letter with a flutter of excitement. He was a little disappointed that it had not been registered. Picking it up, he slid his thumb under the flap and ripped it open, extracted the contents and read the hand-printed scrawl.

'You ask me to send you money under threat of exposure. You suggest a hundred pounds on account and a further hundred every month. I prefer to settle this matter with a lump sum, to be agreed between us, which I will hand over to you at an interview. Be at the corner of Church Street and Creek Road tonight at twelve. I will meet you in a closed car and we can talk without fear of being seen or overheard.'

There was no signature. But no signature was needed, for Mr. Swinger knew very well from whom that letter had emanated.

A lump sum — well, that would suit

him very well. A lump sum could be invested and bring in a steady income. Perhaps, on consideration, it was better than the original arrangement. The monthly payments which he had suggested would cease if anything happened to the man who made them, whereas invested money would yield its dividends regularly and without effort. Yes, a lump sum was preferable.

He poured himself out another cup of the weak tea, added milk and sugar, and lit a cheap cigarette, glancing disparagingly round the cheaply furnished little room. In a few days now he would see the last of this. It was not an environment that appealed to him.

For some time he sat smoking and thinking over his plans for the future, and wondering, as he had wondered so many times before, at the extraordinary luck which had placed this opportunity in his way. From an out-of-work clerk who had never earned more than three pounds ten a week in his life, he would blossom forth into a man of means, able to gratify the little luxuries which his soul had so often craved. And all because he was in possession of knowledge that only one other man in England possessed, knowledge that the police of the whole country wanted to acquire — the identity of the man behind the River Men.

His landlady came to clear away the remains of his meal. 'I have to go out presently, Mrs. Rose,' he said, 'and I'm afraid I shall be rather late; possibly I shall be out until half-past one or two. I'm telling you this in case you should hear me come in and feel nervous.'

She glanced at him in surprise. The curiosity of her class was roused. 'Wherever are you going at that time of night, Mr. Swinger?' she asked.

'I have to meet a man on business,' he answered glibly, 'up west. The business is in connection with an all-night club and that's the only time I could see him.'

'One of these 'ere night clubs, you mean?' said Mrs. Rose, accepting his explanation without question. 'I've 'eard of 'em but I've never been to one — not that I want to,' she added. 'I don't 'old with such things, turnin' night into day and dancin' and drinkin' until the small hours. Are you thinkin' of gettin' a job in one of them places?'

'One has to take what work one can,' said Mr. Swinger without answering the question directly, and she agreed. 'I shall probably be moving next week,' he went on. 'Out of the neighbourhood altogether.'

'Well, I shall be sorry to lose you,' said Mrs. Rose, 'but I suppose if you're goin' to work at such outlandish hours you'll want to be nearer your job.'

He let her think this, and when she had gone settled down with a book to while away the time until it would be necessary to start out and keep his appointment.

At half-past eleven he laid aside his book, pulled on his shabby overcoat and hat, made his way down the narrow stairs and let himself quietly out of the house. He eyed the dirty little street with displeasure as he passed swiftly along towards a turning that would take him into Evelyn Street and eventually to Creek Road. Well, very soon now he would be able to leave the district for good, and it would not break his heart if he never saw that poky little slum again.

It never crossed his mind that he never *would* see it again, or that the next hour was his last on earth. Full of pleasurable anticipation and dreams for the future, he hurried on through the dark streets — to his death.

13

Catherine Acquires an Admirer

Catherine Lee had been back at work for three days before she saw anything further of Terry Ward. For some reason or other, this made her a little resentful. Although she told herself that she was being ridiculous, it annoyed her to think that the young inspector should treat her adventure so casually that he had not taken the trouble to inquire after her health. Had she but known it, she was scarcely ever out of Terry's mind; but he had been so busy, and his time had been so fully occupied, that he had been unable to spare even the half-hour necessary to make a call at Messrs. Macintyre and Sloan.

Her attitude, too, on the morning he had questioned her at the hospital to which she had been taken was still worrying him. That she had been concealing something he was certain, and for the life of him he could not fathom why.

Roy Hugh Macintyre had telephoned that morning to say that he would not be in, and Catherine was busily working at her little desk when there came a tap at the door and a big, rather flashily dressed man entered.

'Good afternoon, my dear,' he said with a pronounced American accent as Catherine looked round. 'I want to see Macintyre. Just tell him I'm here, will you?'

'I'm afraid Mr. Macintyre's not in,' she said, flushing under the boldly admiring eye he turned on her.

'I guess that's too bad. When's he likely to be back?'

'I don't know,' she answered. 'I'm not sure that he's coming in at all today.'

The man's black brows drew together in a frown. 'He made a date — ' he began, and then eyeing her sharply, 'You're not stallin', are you?'

'What do you mean?'

'He didn't tell you to say he was out,

just to put me off?'

'No,' she said shortly. 'When I tell you that Mr. Macintyre's not in, I'm speaking the truth. Perhaps you'd care to see Mr. Swann — '

'My business is with Macintyre,' he interrupted. 'I don't know anything about Swann; he's no good to me. Macintyre's the man I want to see.'

'If you'll leave your name, I'll tell Mr. Macintyre you called.'

He considered this. 'Tell him Jack Renfrew wants to see him,' he said after a pause, 'and the next time he makes a date, to keep it! You can tell 'im that if he thinks I'm the sort of fellow who'll stand for any nonsense, he's mistaken.'

Catherine regarded him with added interest. So this coarse-featured man was a relation of the exotic lady who had called a few mornings before. She decided mentally that they made a good pair. 'I'll give Mr. Macintyre your message immediately he comes in,' she said.

'That's right. Tell him to phone the Chatterton Hotel.' He took a cigar from his waistcoat pocket, bit off the end and lighted it, omitting to remove the band. 'Pretty dull for a woman like you, cooped up all day in this place, isn't it?' he remarked.

'There are worse things,' retorted Catherine.

'What do you do with yourself of an evening? Got a sweetie, I suppose?'

'If by 'sweetie' you mean sweetheart,' replied Catherine coolly, 'I have not yet acquired that doubtful asset.'

Renfrew grinned. 'Must be somethin' wrong with the men in this country,' he remarked. 'Ain't they got any eyes?'

'It takes two to make a bargain, and I'm rather difficult to please.'

His smile broadened, showing his prominent teeth. 'Cute, eh?' he said admiringly. 'Well, I guess you're right. A woman like you don't need to take up with the first fellow who suggests a movie show. Out for somethin' better, eh?'

'Movie shows never did appeal to me, and if I want to go to one I prefer to go by myself.'

The big man chuckled. 'But you wouldn't say no to a nice little dinner up west with a theatre show to follow?' he suggested.

Catherine eyed him calmly. 'That would entirely depend on who asked me. I should say that I never dine out anywhere except at the Carlton, and that a box is the only place in a theatre that appeals to me.'

He uttered a low whistle. 'Expensive tastes, eh? Well, I don't blame you. You're not the fifty-cent type. I'll spring a dinner at the Carlton and a box at any theatre you like to name. What about it?'

'When?'

He thought for a moment. 'What about tomorrow night?' he suggested.

'I'll meet you in the vestibule of the Carlton at seven-thirty,' she answered. 'And now, if you don't mind, I've got a lot of work to do.'

'O.K.!' he exclaimed delightedly. 'Seven-thirty tomorrow night at the Carlton it is. Good afternoon, my dear.'

He went away delighted at his conquest, and making a little note of the appointment in a small book which she took from her handbag, Catherine settled down to her interrupted work.

The taxi which had brought him to Messrs. Macintyre and Sloan's carried Mr. Renfrew back to the West End and deposited him at the door of the Chatterton Hotel. A woman who was indolently reading a magazine looked up as he came into the sitting-room of the suite he had engaged.

'Well, did you see him?' she asked.

He threw his overcoat and hat on the settee. 'No,' he answered. 'He was out.'

She uttered an exclamation of annoyance. 'But he made the appointment!' she protested. 'When he was here the other night — '

'I know all that,' said her husband impatiently. 'But I tell you he was out.'

'Or stalling,' she put in quickly.

He shook his head. 'No, he was out sure enough. I saw his stenographer or secretary or whatever she is. Cute bit of goods. I'll say Macintyre's got a mean taste.'

The woman eyed him suspiciously. 'Fallen again?' she inquired sarcastically.

'Don't be silly,' he rejoined. 'Can't I admire a woman without falling for her?'

'It 'ud be a fresh experience! Listen,

Jack, you've got to get hold of Macintyre. We're down to nearly our last dollar, and that fellow's got to part.'

'He'll part, all right. You leave that to me. By the way, I won't be able to go to that dance with you tomorrow. You'll have to find some way of amusing yourself on your own. I've got a business appointment.'

'Who with?' she asked.

'A fellow I met this morning,' he answered glibly. 'Somebody I knew in Chicago. Ran into him by accident in Piccadilly Circus, an' he's got a proposition he wants to discuss.'

'Who was it?' she asked again.

'Nobody you know. A fellow I knew years ago.'

The expression on her face showed that she was far from satisfied. 'I suppose it's some woman or other,' she muttered. 'Why don't you keep your mind on business?'

'This *is* business, I tell you,' he answered angrily. 'You're always thinking of women!'

'It's not me who's always thinking of them. Once you get the money from Macintyre, I don't care what you do, you know that. But it's no good wasting time on a parcel of dames when we're broke. You're not taking out that secretary of his, are you?'

'Don't be crazy!' he snapped. 'Why, I've only seen the woman once.'

'You're a fast worker. Well, you can do what you like, only don't forget we've got to have that money. They sent up the bill this morning.' She jerked her head towards a small table near the window, and he picked up the paper that lay there.

'Gosh!' he muttered. 'They know how to charge, these guys!'

'Well, you can't stay at a place like this without paying for it. And it was you who suggested we should come to a grand place like the Chatterton.'

'Sure,' he agreed. 'What does it matter? Micky'll find the dough, he promised — '

'He promised he'd see you this morning, and he hasn't kept it. He's a smart guy, Jack, and we've got to watch out. If he gets a chance to double-cross us, he'll do it.'

'What chance has he got?' said the man, shrugging his shoulders. 'He's on the hook and he can't wriggle off. Maybe he had to go somewhere important this morning. I'll ring him at his flat tonight.'

'And don't forget we want cash,' she said warningly.

'Sure. I'm not accepting any cheques. We'll get cash. I tell you, that fellow won't dare to do anything. We've got him just where we want him. If he don't come up to scratch — well, a letter sent to police headquarters here 'ull cook his goose. Don't you worry, Marion, Micky'll part all right. He knows we've got the whip hand.'

The woman made no reply. A sixth sense, or maybe just her native intuition, was making her uneasy. Macintyre had seemed tractable enough when they had discussed the matter at dinner, but she was by no means certain that this tractability was genuine. At the back of her mind she had a feeling that Macintyre was not such easy prey as she had imagined.

And she was right. The new head of Messrs. Macintyre and Sloan was a dangerous man to threaten. His adventurous life had landed him in many tight corners, and he was never so formidable as when he fought with his back against the wall. At that first interview, Roy Macintyre had decided that he had no intention of supplying the Renfrews with easy money, and his plans had been laid carefully to obviate any such unpleasant contingency.

14

The Man in the Boat

The captain of a Dutch barge who, being unable to sleep, had come up from his quarters for a smoke and a breath of fresh air, saw the dinghy drifting downstream and thought it was empty, as did a watchman on a fruit boat lower down-river.

It is not unusual for small craft to break away during the night, and neither of these two thought any more about it, except that the watchman wondered vaguely to whom it belonged and where it would land.

It was captured eventually by a river patrol in the vicinity of Gallions Reach, and like the captain of the barge and the watchman, he, too, thought it was empty, until a closer inspection revealed the grim thing that lay sprawled on the bottom.

The find was taken in tow and brought

to a riverside station, where it was examined more carefully. The dead man who lay crumpled up in the bottom of the boat was of medium height and shabbily dressed. His pale face was undistinguished, and there was nothing upon him to reveal his identity. He had died from a knife-thrust in the side, but there was no sign of a weapon, and although the blood had soaked into his clothing, there were no stains in the boat.

'Looks as though he was killed and put in the boat after,' said the inspector who conducted the examination. 'There's no doubt it was murder. Who does the dinghy belong to?'

This was a difficult question to answer, for there was nothing on the little boat to betray its ownership. It was old and battered, and the oars belonging to it were missing.

The dead man was removed to the mortuary and a search instituted for the owner of the boat. Many wearisome inquiries were made by patient men working slowly upstream, and eventually the dinghy was identified as having belonged to a wharf near the Royal Naval College at Greenwich. The owners of the wharf kept the boat for the purpose of ferrying and other odd jobs, and it had been missed when the men arrived to begin work that morning.

The matter had been reported to the manager, and he had come to the conclusion that it had either been insecurely tied or had broken away, and given the matter very little further thought, for the dinghy was an old one and of small value. He was pleased when he learned that it had been found, but horrified when the nature of its contents was made known to him.

'A dead man?' he gasped. 'Good Lord! How did he come to be in our boat?'

'That's what we're trying to discover, sir,' said the patient sergeant who was making the inquiries, 'Perhaps you'll come down to the station and see if you can identify him.'

The manager reluctantly accompanied him, but shook his head when he was shown the pathetic remains. 'Never seen him before in my life,' he averred. 'He's a complete stranger to me.' He left the mortuary paler than when he had entered it, and after complying with certain formalities which were necessary, hurried back to his work.

The police could do nothing more than follow the usual routine, and this they did. Notification of the discovery was sent to Scotland Yard and a description of the man and the manner of his death circulated.

Terry Ward was interested, and suggested a theory to his immediate superior.

'Nonsense!' scoffed that grey-haired veteran. 'You've got the River Men on the brain! Anyway, this wasn't a river crime at all. The boat was only used as a means of disposing of the body. He was killed somewhere else.'

His words were borne out by the discovery of a policeman patrolling a lonely part of Blackheath. Almost hidden amongst some bushes, the constable came upon an abandoned car, the front seat of which was badly stained with blood. He reported his discovery, and inquiries were instituted at the County Hall concerning the ownership of the machine. It proved to have belonged to a major in the Guards who had reported its loss on the previous night. He had left it unattended in Half Moon Street while visiting a friend, and when he had come out of the block of flats the car had vanished.

It was examined carefully for any clues that might lead to the identity of the thief, but none was found. The only fingerprints were those of its legitimate owner.

'Unless there was another murder committed here last night,' said the superintendent at Wapping, 'it was in that car that our unknown man was killed.'

Terry agreed with him. The body being discovered in the drifting boat had brought the murder into the province of the river police, but since the crime had apparently been committed inland, it was also a matter for the attention of the land men. Terry was sent for by Scotland Yard, and went to interview Chief Inspector Ransom.

'D'you think this crime has got anything to do with the River Gang?' asked Ransom when the young inspector was seated in his cheerless office. 'Or is it just an ordinary murder?'

'I've got a hunch the River Men are at the bottom of it,' answered Terry, 'but my superintendent doesn't agree with me.'

'Any reason for thinking so?'

'No definite reason.'

'Hm! Well, it's difficult to say,' said the chief inspector, fingering his chin. 'The obvious thing to do is to discover the identity of the dead man; that may help us a lot.'

It helped them considerably, though the knowledge didn't reach them till the following day when an agitated woman called at the police station in Blackheath Road and made a statement. Mrs. Rose was tearful and a little incoherent, but her information proved invaluable.

'I'm sure it's Mr. Swinger,' she said. 'The description fits him to a T, and he ain't been 'ome since he went out the night before last.'

They listened to what she had to say and took her, protesting, to the mortuary. At sight of the dead man she fainted, but when the police surgeon had succeeded in bringing her round she was emphatic.

'That's 'im,' she wailed. 'I knew no good 'ud come of 'is getting 'isself mixed up with these 'ere night clubs.'

She was questioned further and told her story. Terry, accompanied by an inspector from the Blackheath Station, returned with her to her home and instituted a search of the room which her late lodger had occupied. Crumpled up in the fireplace he found the letter which had taken Mr. Swinger to his death.

'Here we are,' he said, showing it to his confrere. 'Here's the motive. This fellow Swinger was putting the black on somebody. The fellow he was blackmailing made this appointment to meet him at the corner of Church Street and Creek Road, arrived in the stolen car, killed him, got rid of the body by putting it in the boat and turning it adrift, and then abandoned the car on Blackheath.'

'That's right,' agreed the inspector stolidly. 'All we want now is the name of the fellow who did him in.'

Terry looked at him sharply but his face was expressionless, and if he was endeavouring to get a rise out of the river man, there was no sign of it on his wooden features.

'That's all we want,' he said. 'Perhaps it isn't going to be so easy. This fellow Swinger wasn't a habitual criminal. His fingerprints have been up to the Yard and they've got nothing like 'em in Records.'

'I should say this was his first assay into crime — and the last, poor devil,' said the land man. 'He was unlucky.'

They sent for Mrs. Rose and questioned her concerning all she knew about her late lodger.

'He was a very quiet, 'ard-working feller,' she said. 'And while 'e had a job, the rent was always regular. It was only lately, since 'e's been out of work, that he got be'ind, and I didn't worry much 'cause I knew he'd settle up soon as he got fixed 'imself again.'

'Who did he work for?' asked Terry; he was unprepared for her answer.

'He used to be an invoice clerk at Macintyre and Sloan's,' she replied. 'You know, the shipping people in Butcher Road.'

'I know them very well,' said Terry

softly. 'So Swinger used to work for Macintyre and Sloan, did he.'

'That's right. He was sacked when this new feller came, 'im what in'erited the business from his uncle. He got rid of a lot of the old staff when he came, and Mr. Swinger was one of them.'

'I see,' said Terry absently, and he was thinking rapidly.

Macintyre had a flat in Swallow Street, not a stone's throw from where the car had been stolen. The corner of Creek Road and Church Street was within walking distance of the warehouse, and the wharf from which the boat had been turned adrift containing Swinger's body was close, too. Macintyre would be well aware that a boat was kept there . . .

'Well, we didn't learn much,' grunted the inspector as after a number of further questions they took their leave. 'It looks as though we shall have to try a new tack.'

'We didn't learn much,' said Terry, 'but I think we learned enough.'

His companion eyed him in astonishment. 'What do you mean?' he asked. 'Do you mean something the old woman told

169

us has given you a clue?'

'Not exactly a clue,' Terry answered cautiously. 'But I should very much like to know where Roy Macintyre, of Macintyre and Sloan, was from eleven o'clock until one on the night that fellow Swinger met his death.'

15

Macintyre's Alibi

Mr. Macintyre was in a villainous temper. He had arrived early at the office, and when Catherine had taken in his letters, he had greeted her with a scowl on his dark face, acknowledging her 'Good morning' with an unintelligible grunt. He had not put in an appearance at all on the previous day, and in spite of his absence from work looked tired and worn.

'Oh, Mr. Macintyre,' she said as she was leaving the inner office, 'a gentleman called here yesterday morning to see you, a Mr. Renfrew. He said he had an appointment.'

His frown deepened. 'I forgot,' he growled. 'Did he leave any message?'

'Only would you ring him up at the Chatterton Hotel,' she answered.

'You're sure he said nothing else?' Macintyre eyed her keenly.

'No. Did you expect him to leave any other message?'

'I just wanted to know, that's all,' he said irritably. 'And while I remember it, Miss Lee, if anyone comes here while I'm out, asking you questions or talking about me, you know nothing. You understand?'

She looked at him in surprise. 'I shouldn't dream of discussing you,' she said quietly.

'That's all right,' he said, and jerked his head in dismissal. 'Women chatter about all sorts of things.'

'I'm not one of those women!' she retorted, and went into her own office before he could think of anything more unpleasant.

For some time after she had gone, he sat at his desk fidgeting with a pencil, his unlooked-at mail at his elbow. Then abruptly rising to his feet, he lit a cigarette, walked over to the window, and stood staring gloomily out at the river.

Things were becoming a great deal more involved than he had expected. The advent of the Renfrews had upset him considerably, and although he had perfected his plans for dealing with them, he was not feeling any too easy in his mind. Perhaps the best thing to do would be to stage a big coup and get away while the going was good. The last few days had brought more shocks than he liked.

He came back to the desk and, sitting down, forced himself to take an interest in the letters and documents Catherine had put in readiness for his perusal. There were no private letters for his attention, and he had just finished making a pencilled note on the last when Catherine came in to announce that Inspector Ward wished to see him. Macintyre suppressed the start that the name induced and hoped he looked better than he felt.

'That fellow here again? What does he want this time?'

If she noticed any outward trace of his agitation, she gave no sign. 'I don't know. He just asked if he could see you.'

Macintyre rubbed his chin. 'I suppose I'd better see him. All right, shoot him in.'

'Well,' he greeted as Terry entered, 'what have you found this time?'

There was a sneer in his voice, and the

young inspector sensed the hostility in the atmosphere.

'I haven't found anything, Mr. Macintyre,' he said quietly. 'I've called to ask if you could give me any information concerning a man called Swinger, who I believe was at one time in your employ.'

'Swinger?' repeated Macintyre, pursing his lips and frowning. 'I don't recollect the name. What was he?'

'One of your invoice clerks.'

'Don't remember him. I made a lot of changes when I took over here. The majority of the staff had gone slack and I sacked several of them. Why don't you see Swann? He'd know more than me. He's in closer contact with these people.'

'I should like to see your general manager later.'

'Why are you inquiring about this man, what's-his-name — Swinger?' asked Macintyre. 'What's he done?'

'He hasn't done anything,' said Terry quietly. 'He's dead.'

He watched the man behind the desk closely, but if he expected to see any change in the dark face at his words, he was disappointed. Beyond a slight raising of his eyebrows, Macintyre's face was expressionless.

'Why have you come to me?' he demanded. 'Why should I take any interest in the death of a discharged employee?'

'Because,' snapped Terry, 'everybody takes an interest in wilful murder, and Swinger was stabbed to death the night before last in a stolen motorcar and his body put in a boat and turned adrift.'

Once again he searched for some sign of emotion in the face of the man before him, but not a muscle moved.

'I read about that,' said Macintyre coolly. 'Was that Swinger? Well, I know nothing about the man. I'm sorry, but I can't help you.'

'The car, in which we have reason to believe he was murdered,' said Terry, 'was stolen from outside a block of flats in Half Moon Street.' He paused.

'Well, what about it?' said Macintyre.

'You have a flat in Swallow Street, just round the corner.'

The hard, cold eyes narrowed. 'Quite a number of people have flats in that

175

district. Am I to understand, Inspector, that you suspect me of having stolen this car and killed the man?'

Terry evaded a direct reply. Whatever he might suspect, he had no evidence as yet to warrant accusing this man, and the regulations concerning the conduct of a police officer in making his inquiries were very strict. A slight mistake and he would lay himself open to a severe reprimand from his superiors.

'I'm sure you will realize, Mr. Macintyre,' he said, 'that in the investigation of wilful murder we have to interview and question a number of people. The dead man, Swinger, was once in your employ and therefore, naturally, you come on our list. It's been discovered that Swinger was blackmailing someone, and that this someone made an appointment by letter to meet him in a closed car at the corner of Church Street and Creek Road. That car was undoubtedly the one stolen from Half Moon Street, and Swinger was killed in the vehicle. You'll help us considerably if you'd give an account of your movements between the hours of half-past ten and one on the night in question.'

'Supposing I refuse,' said Macintyre coolly. 'I fail to recognize your right to question me, Inspector, concerning my movements.'

'There's nothing to prevent you refusing, sir. I can't force you to answer. But I should warn you that you can be subpoenaed as a witness at the inquest, and then these questions I'm asking you privately will be put to you by the coroner in public.'

Macintyre considered. 'Well, I've nothing to hide. I assure you, Inspector, that I had nothing to do with this man's death. I don't even remember what he was like or anything about him. Whoever he was blackmailing, it wasn't me.' He took his case from his pocket, lit a cigarette, and leaning back in his chair blew a stream of smoke towards the ceiling. 'Let me see if I can remember,' he murmured, 'what I was doing on the night before last. Oh, yes, of course! I dined at home and went to a theatre. I left at ten minutes past eleven and had supper at a small restaurant in Soho. I can't remember the name of it; it was a place I've not been to before. After that, feeling the need of a little exercise, I went for a walk, reaching my flat somewhere around half-past twelve or maybe a quarter to one. Then I went to bed.'

'What was the name of the theatre you went to?'

'The Coronet,' replied Macintyre promptly. 'I decided to go during the afternoon and rang up from this office to book a seat.' He smiled mirthlessly. 'You should have no difficulty, Inspector, in confirming my statement, for I booked the seat in my own name and arranged for it to be left at the box office for me to call.'

Terry made a mental note to inquire at the box office of the Coronet.

'So you see,' continued Macintyre, 'that if this car you mention was stolen before eleven, it couldn't have been stolen by me, for at that time I was in the Coronet Theatre.'

There was truth in this, and Terry was a little nonplussed. The rest of Macintyre's alibi, however, was not so convincing. It would be difficult to check up on his subsequent movements after leaving the theatre. For the hundredth time, he cursed the luck that had removed the watcher who had been put on to trail Macintyre on the very night when he would have been most useful. There had been a big raid on a spieling house in the West End that night, and every available man who could be spared had been put on to deal with it, including the man who had been keeping Macintyre under observation.

Macintyre saw his frown and his thin lips curled. 'I'm afraid, Inspector,' he said smoothly, 'that you'll have to postpone the pleasure of arresting me for a crime I didn't commit.'

Terry's mouth tightened. 'There was no question of arrest, Mr. Macintyre. I'm merely following up a routine inquiry.'

'So far as I'm concerned, you've been wasting your time!'

And on this note, the interview terminated.

Terry paused in the outer office to have a word with Catherine. He thought she looked a little pale and worried, and put this down to the after-effects of her unpleasant adventure.

An inquiry at the Coronet Theatre confirmed Macintyre's statement. He had rung up in the afternoon for a stall, which had been kept for him in accordance with the theatre's regulations until seven-thirty. The ticket had been used, but the box office keeper could not remember what the man was like who had called for it. The result of this inquiry showed that someone had occupied the seat booked by Macintyre, but there was no evidence to prove that this was Macintyre himself, nor was there any evidence to show that it was not. The man's alibi was by no means watertight. In fact, it was scarcely an alibi at all; but unless something further came to light implicating him in the death of Swinger, it was impossible to take any action.

Terry went home a little depressed and out of sorts. He was convinced in his own mind that Macintyre was the prime mover behind the River Men, and fairly certain that he was deeply implicated in the murder of Swinger. But there was no proof, and so far as he could see, no proof was obtainable.

Dusk had fallen as he turned into the quiet street in which he lived, and he was walking slowly towards his house when he saw a man on a bicycle coming towards him. He took little notice of the cyclist beyond seeing that he was crouching low over his handlebars, and the man had passed him before he heard the dull 'plop' of a silenced pistol and the wind of a bullet fanned his cheek.

In an instant he had swung round, but the cyclist was pedalling furiously away and was already almost out of sight.

Terry looked at the chipped mark on a brick pillar where the bullet had struck, and his face was set. This was the second attempt on his life, and it was peculiar that, like the first, it had followed closely on an interview with Macintyre . . .

He entered the little gate of his house and let himself in with a very thoughtful expression on his face.

16

The Tragedy at Chatterton

Punctually at half-past six, Catherine Lee put the cover on her typewriter, tidied her desk, and prepared herself for the street. She was a little annoyed, for she was later than usual in leaving the office, and she had wished to be early. But at the last moment, Macintyre had called her in and dictated several urgent letters that he wanted done at once, and these had kept her.

He was still in his office when she left, but the rest of the staff had gone. She hurried along Butcher Road and up Watergate Street, for this evening was the evening of her appointment with Mr. Renfrew, and she had very little time in which to dress and reach the Carlton. She was not looking forward to her evening with any degree of pleasurable anticipation.

She frowned as she let herself into her lodgings and hurried up the stairs to her little room, and was still there when half an hour later she emerged, her evening cloak wrapped round her, and made her way in search of a taxi. It was twenty minutes to eight when she reached the Carlton, and looking round the vestibule, she discovered that her escort had not yet arrived. Finding a vacant chair, she sat down and waited, her eyes on the entrance. The time crept slowly by, but the coarse-faced American did not put in an appearance.

Catherine began to feel, not unreasonably, annoyed. The appointment had been definite and she had had no misgivings that it would not be kept.

A quarter to eight — ten minutes to eight.

At eight o'clock, she glanced at the little jewelled watch on her wrist and rose to her feet. She had waited over twenty minutes, and she was not going to wait any longer. Either the man had forgotten the appointment or something had prevented him coming.

She sent the commissionaire for a taxi,

and was standing under the portico waiting for its arrival when a man passed her, walking rapidly up the Haymarket. Something familiar about his appearance attracted her attention, and she was looking after him when he turned and glanced back. It was Jimmy Swann!

He hesitated, stopped, and then, as she smiled her recognition, came towards her.

'Why, Miss Lee,' he said, lifting his hat. 'I thought it was you, but I felt sure I must be mistaken.'

'You've made no mistake, Mr. Swann.' She smiled. 'You behold in me a disappointed female whose cavalier for the evening has failed to keep his appointment!'

He looked a little puzzled. She noted, rather surprised, that he was in evening dress, though it struck her afterwards that there was no reason why this should have astonished her. She had no knowledge of Jimmy S's private life, and there was nothing peculiar in the fact that he should take a little amusement.

'You mean,' he said, 'that the person you were going to meet has not turned up?'

'I mean just that,' she answered. 'I've been left flat; hungry, cold, and very annoyed.'

'You were dining here?' His eyes surveyed the dignified entrance to the Carlton.

She nodded. 'I was. But now I shall go home.'

The taxi which the commissionaire had ordered at her request had drawn up to the kerb, and the man was looking towards her expectantly.

'Would you — would you — ' He was a little embarrassed. 'Would you care to accept me as a substitute for the ungallant gentleman who let you down?' he asked diffidently. 'I — I'm afraid I can't run to the Carlton, but . . . ' he stammered and reddened.

'I'm not even superior to a tea shop,' she said with a smile. 'Thank you, Mr. Swann, it's very nice of you.' His face lighted up.

'It's very nice of *you*,' he said, and looking round. 'Is this your taxi?'

She nodded.

'Let's go then,' he suggested; and as they crossed the strip of pavement, the commissionaire held open the door. Catherine got in, and Swann turned to the man and slipped a coin into his ready palm. 'Chatterton Hotel,' he said, and she heard the direction with something like dismay. What had made him choose the Chatterton, of all places? A protest rose to her lips, but it was never uttered. It occurred to her that it would be amusing after all to go to the Chatterton, particularly if the discourteous Mr. Renfrew happened to be dining there.

Jimmy S took his seat beside her, and the taxi moved off. 'I hope you don't object to the Chatterton?' he remarked. 'The manager is a friend of mine, and whenever I do have a little evening in town, which is not very often, I usually go there. The food is very good and the place is quiet and select.'

It was also very expensive, she thought, but did not mention this. Presumably, being a friend of the management, Jimmy S did not have to pay the prices charged to the other habitués, for a meal at the Chatterton at normal charges would have come no cheaper than the Carlton.

He must have guessed what was passing in her mind, for he said, rather apologetically: 'You see, they allow me fifty percent off the bill.'

The cab drew up at the unpretentious entrance to the hotel, and a uniformed porter hurried down the shallow steps to open the door. Jimmy Swann got out and assisted Catherine to alight. She entered the small, rather sombre vestibule while he settled with the driver, and glanced around her, for she had never been to the Chatterton before.

There was nothing of the plaster and gilt type of decoration about the Chatterton. The foyer was panelled in polished oak and lit with soft shaded lights. In one corner was a small counter behind which a spectacled reception clerk pored over a ledger. There was an atmosphere of exclusiveness and, she thought with a twitch of her lips, dullness.

Jimmy S joined her, giving his coat and hat to the attendant who hurried forward, and they passed through the swing doors at the back of the lounge into the dining-room, a long, low-roofed room panelled in faded brocade, each snowy table lit by its own silk-shaded lamp.

James Swann was evidently well known, for the head waiter came forward to greet them with a smile. 'Good evening, Mr. Swann,' he said, bowing to Catherine. 'It's a long time since you've been here, sir.'

Jimmy S murmured something, and the man led the way to a secluded table in a corner and pulled out two chairs. Catherine sank into one of them and unfastened her cloak. While Jimmy S consulted the menu and gave his order, she glanced round the room. Few of the tables were occupied, and there was no sign of the red-faced Mr. Renfrew.

Jimmy S chose the dinner with care and, she was surprised to discover, with insight. When the waiter had left them, the manager turned to her with a smile.

'This is the greatest and most unexpected piece of luck that has ever come my way, Miss Lee,' he said. 'I was looking forward to a lonely evening, and lo, the fates have been kind.'

'They have certainly been kind to me,' she answered, and he flushed with pleasure.

'Have you ever been here before?' he

asked, and when she shook her head: 'I like it because it's quiet. One can get good food without the accompaniment of bad music.'

'Do you come here often?'

'No,' he answered, twisting the stem of his glass. 'My salary at Macintyre and Sloan's does not permit of a too frequent indulgence in these sort of things. My average appearance at the Chatterton is once a month.'

The wine waiter bustled up, and Jimmy S consulted the list with knitted brows. The order he gave caused Catherine to turn to him with a protest. 'You really shouldn't have been so extravagant,' she murmured. 'I'd just as soon have had something cheaper.'

He waved aside her protest with a smile. 'This is an occasion, Miss Lee,' he said. 'It's very seldom that I have the opportunity of entertaining a charming young lady.'

She flushed at the admiration in his eyes and was silent, a little embarrassed and perturbed. He must have seen her unease, for he began to talk about a number of commonplace things until, by the arrival of the soup, she had forgotten her momentary disquiet.

During the meal that followed, she discovered that Jimmy S could be very entertaining in his quiet way. He was a well-read man, and had interesting views on a variety of subjects. He appeared to have got over his initial shyness, and betrayed an unexpected sense of humour that kept Catherine in a constant ripple of soft laughter.

They had reached the coffee stage before they became aware of the excitement that was going on around them. It was Jimmy S who first noticed it, and drew Catherine's attention to the fact. 'What's up, I wonder?' he muttered. 'Something unusual by the look of things.'

The fat-faced manager had hurried agitatedly through the long room, his brow wrinkled and worried, barely acknowledging Jimmy Swann's nod of greeting. The head waiter was whispering excitedly to one of his underlings, and a sudden air of tension had replaced the soothing quiet which was such a feature of the Chatterton.

The manager reappeared through the little door at the end of the room, and as he drew near their table, Jimmy Swann called to him. He came over quickly.

'You must excuse me, Mr. Swann,' he said jerkily. 'I cannot stop.' His eyes were on the swing doors leading to the lounge; he was obviously anxious to get away.

'What's the matter, Rimini?' asked Jimmy S.

Monsieur Rimini glanced round quickly. 'A dreadful thing has 'appened,' he said in a low voice. 'I do not want any of my guests to know. A terrible thing! The hotel will be ruined!'

Swann raised his eyebrows. 'Has the chef poisoned somebody?' he asked quizzically.

The manager shook his head. 'It is nothing to joke about, Mr. Swann,' he said. 'It is not — what you call it? — funny. Two of my guests, two people who are staying at the hotel, have died. I have sent for the police; they are here now.'

Swann's expression changed. 'Died?' he said. 'D'you mean committed suicide?'

Again the stout manager shook his head. 'No, no! More serious than that. It is, we think — murder!' He spoke the sinister word in so low a tone that they

191

scarcely caught it.

'Murder!' Jimmy S pursed his lips. 'That's going to be a serious thing for you, Rimini.'

'Serious?' The manager spread out his hands in a gesture. 'Monsieur, it is ruin! Our clients are select. The best people, you understand? They will not come to a place that is — what you say? — in the limelight.'

'Who were the people killed?' asked Catherine. She never knew what prompted her to ask the question.

Monsieur Rimini hesitated. 'There is no reason why you should not be told,' he said after a pause. 'It will be in all the papers, it is sure to be in all the papers. An American couple who have been staying with us for the past fortnight.'

Catherine stared at him, and the horror in her eyes was apparent. 'Not — not Mr. and Mrs. Renfrew?' she breathed.

The manager nodded. 'Yes, yes! That was their name. Did you know them?'

'No, I knew *of* them,' she replied. 'When — when did this happen?'

'The discovery was made half an hour

ago, but the doctor says they had been dead two hours.'

Catherine was silent. The reason why Jack Renfrew had not kept his appointment at the Carlton was obvious. At seven-thirty he was dead!

17

The Parcel

Chief Inspector Ransom was visiting his area when the news came through from the agitated manager of the Chatterton, and elected to accompany the divisional inspector on his inquiries.

Standing now in the beautiful suite which the unfortunate Renfrew and his wife had occupied, he puzzled over the mysterious affair, going over in his mind the meagre information the police had succeeded in acquiring.

The tragedy had been discovered by a waiter, and this man had been interviewed. Renfrew had apparently ordered coffee for his wife to be brought at eight-thirty, when the floor waiter had come earlier to clear away the tea which he had had sent up to their sitting-room. The man had forgotten all about the order until five minutes past nine, when he had suddenly remembered. Going down to the kitchen, he had ordered the coffee and hastily carried it upstairs. He had received no answer to his first knock, nor to his second, and concluding that perhaps the occupants were in the inner bedroom, had opened the door and gone in.

Renfrew, partially dressed in trousers and shirt, was lying midway between the door and the settee; his wife was crumpled up in a chair nearby.

The shock had been so great that the waiter had almost dropped the tray he was carrying, but he was a man not without presence of mind, and quickly seeing that something was seriously wrong, had informed the manager. In his statement, he mentioned that he had noticed a peculiar smell in the apartment; a faint acrid chemical-like smell that had caused him to conclude, not unreasonably, that the couple had committed suicide, for it was obvious even to his non-technical eyes that they were both dead.

The police doctor's examination accounted for this peculiar odour. Death had been caused by inhalation of phosgene gas, a virulent poison, the slightest whiff of which was fatal. The means by which this gas had been introduced to the apartment was quickly discovered. By the side of the chair in which the woman lay had been found a freshly opened parcel. It consisted of a square box inside which lay a shattered glass flask — an oblong container not unlike the interior of a thermos bottle. The box had a hinged lid, and attached to this was a simple mechanism that on examination proved to have been constructed so that anyone opening the lid would cause the breakage of the glass, releasing the deadly fumes that the flask had held.

'Ingenious!' murmured Ransom when he saw this. 'And a new one on me. I've seen all sorts of bombs and infernal machines, but nothing like this before.' The divisional inspector, to whom he made the remark, agreed.

'The thing is, who sent it?' he said.

'That's the thing, as you say,' Ransom remarked. 'Evidently someone who had a pretty serious grudge against these two.'

Inquiry elicited the fact that the box, wrapped in brown paper and addressed to Mrs. Renfrew, had been delivered by district messenger at the Chatterton Hotel shortly after seven. The attendant had brought it up to their apartment and she had taken it in.

'It shouldn't be difficult to trace that district messenger,' said the divisional inspector hopefully.

Ransom shrugged his shoulders. 'Unless the person who killed these people is a fool — and the method he used seems to prove that he isn't — I doubt if we shall learn much if we do trace the messenger,' he said. 'Get that fat manager in here, I want to talk to him.'

Monsieur Rimini was sent for, and came, a worried and greatly agitated man. 'It is a terrible thing!' he wailed. 'A dreadful catastrophe! The hotel will never recover. They had not paid their bill, either — '

'Yes, yes,' broke in Ransom soothingly. 'I understand how you feel, Monsieur Rimini, and you have my sympathy. The important thing at the moment, however, is to discover who is responsible for this crime. What do you know about these people?'

The manager shrugged his shoulders and spread his hands. 'Me? I know nothing,' he declared. 'They were Americans. Three weeks ago they drive up with their luggage and take this apartment. That is all I know about them.'

'Have they had any visitors during their stay?' asked Ransom. 'Any friends to see them?'

Monsieur Rimini began to shake his head and stopped. 'I forget. Yes, they have one gentleman. He came one, two, three, four evenings ago, I think, I cannot be quite certain. He came to dinner with them.'

Ransom looked interested. 'What was this man's name?'

'A Mr. Macintyre.'

The chief inspector uttered a little exclamation.

'A Mr. Macintyre, eh?' he repeated softly. 'That sounds interesting to me. He came to dinner with them, you say?'

Monsieur Rimini nodded.

'And was he the only person who

visited them?' said Ransom.

'I think so. Yes, I am sure. My reception clerk will be able to tell you.'

'I'll see him presently,' said the chief inspector. 'Did these people have many letters?'

Monsieur Rimini shook his head. 'They had no letters. I thought it strange but concluded that it was because they were newcomers to this country. If this gets into the papers, I am ruined! The hotel will get a bad name and nobody will come!'

Ransom dismissed him, still bemoaning his fate, and sent for the reception clerk. This man bore out his employer's statement. The only visitor the Renfrews had had since their stay at the Chatterton was a Mr. Macintyre. They had received no letters, and the reception clerk could offer no information to supplement Monsieur Rimini's.

The police photographers took photographs and the fatal parcel was subjected to a test for fingerprints. On the outer wrapping several were discovered, but on the box only those of the dead woman.

'The man who constructed the death machine must have worn gloves,' said Ransom, and he set about issuing orders for the removal of the bodies.

Monsieur Rimini met him in the vestibule as he was going out, detaching himself with difficulty from a group of newspaper reporters who, by some extraordinary means, had got wind of the affair.

'I have remembered,' said the manager, 'the gentleman, Mr. Macintyre, who called — he is the owner of the firm of shippers and importers — '

'I already know that,' said Ransom shortly, and he made his way to the police car which was drawn up at the kerb.

The distance from the Chatterton to Waverly Mansions was a short one, and five minutes later Ransom got out as the car stopped in the quiet street, and looked round him. A man who was lounging on the opposite side of the road saw him and crossed over.

'Is Macintyre in?' asked the chief inspector.

'Yes, sir. He's been in all evening.'

'What time did he come home?'

'Just after seven. He came straight from the warehouse.'

'Did he stop anywhere on the way?'

The man shook his head. 'No, sir. He got into his car at Butcher Road, drove straight here, and he's been in his flat ever since.'

Ransom was a little disappointed. He had hoped for more valuable information.

'All right. Go back to your post,' he said, and the detective returned to his vigil.

Entering the vestibule, the chief inspector was carried up to the fourth floor, and pausing outside the door of Macintyre's flat, pressed the bell. The door was opened after a slight delay by Mint, who eyed the visitor inquiringly.

'I want to see Mr. Macintyre,' said Ransom shortly. 'Take this card in to him, will you?' He handed the servant an official card and saw the surprise in his eyes as he read the inscription.

'If you'll wait just a moment, sir,' said Mint, 'I'll see if Mr. Macintyre will see you.'

He half closed the door, and crossing

the hall tapped on a door at the far end. Disappearing into the room beyond, he presently came back again, still holding the chief inspector's card in his fingers.

'Mr. Macintyre says will you please state your business, sir?' he said. 'He's very busy and doesn't wish to be disturbed.'

'I'm afraid he'll have to be, all the same,' said Ransom. 'Tell him I'm afraid I can't state my business, but it's most urgent that I should see him.'

Once again Mint went away, and after a longer interval than before came back with the information that Mr. Macintyre could give the chief inspector five minutes. He ushered him into the study, and Macintyre, sitting behind the big desk, looked up from a litter of papers as he entered.

'Really, this is getting intolerable!' he said angrily. 'I'm continuously pestered by an inspector of the river police at my office, and now I cannot spend a quiet evening at home without being interrupted. What is it you want?'

'Some information, sir,' said Ransom

smoothly, and he waited until the door had closed behind the obviously interested Mint.

'Information?' Macintyre leaned back in his chair and his frown deepened. 'Information concerning what?'

'Information concerning a Mr. and Mrs. Renfrew,' answered the chief inspector, eyeing the other keenly. But the only expression on Macintyre's sallow face was one of surprise.

'Mr. and Mrs. Renfrew,' he said, and shook his head. 'I know very little about them.'

'Yet I believe you dined with them at the Chatterton Hotel a few nights ago.'

'Yes, that's perfectly true,' answered Macintyre, returning his gaze steadily. 'I dine with a good many people, Inspector. What is the object of these inquiries?'

'The object, sir,' said Ransom curtly, 'is to discover who was responsible for their deaths.'

Macintyre's face was the picture of astonishment. 'Their deaths?' he echoed. 'What do you mean?'

'I mean,' said Chief Inspector Ransom

rapidly, 'that Mr. and Mrs. Renfrew were murdered in their apartment at the Chatterton Hotel at a little after seven this evening!'

'Good God, you horrify me!' exclaimed Macintyre. 'Are you serious?'

'I'm very serious, sir. Long years in the police force may have hardened me, but I have yet to see anything amusing in wilful murder.'

'How did it happen?' Macintyre rose to his feet and walked to the fireplace.

'They were poisoned by means of a gas which was liberated by an ingenious contrivance contained in a parcel sent to them. We're trying to trace the sender of that parcel.'

'And you suspect me?' Macintyre took up the challenge coolly. 'It's a remarkable thing, Inspector, but apparently when any unusual incident occurs, the police immediately suspect me as being responsible for it.'

'Maybe they have reason!' retorted Ransom. 'Inquiries have elicited the fact, sir, that you were the only person apparently on friendly terms with these people.'

'I knew them,' agreed Macintyre. 'I met them once or twice in America. But to say that I *knew* them is an exaggeration. I knew nothing about them, if that's what you mean.'

'Can you give me the name of anyone else they were acquainted with in England?'

'No, I'm afraid I can't. I knew them slightly in America, and a few days ago Mrs. Renfrew called at my office. I was surprised to see her because I had no idea that she and her husband were in England. She invited me to dine with them at the Chatterton, and having nothing to do that evening, I accepted. That's all I can tell you.'

This was little enough, as Ransom had to admit. 'You know of nobody,' he said, 'who might have reason to wish these people harm?'

Macintyre shook his head. 'Isn't it possible — I'm not trying to do your work for you, Inspector — but isn't it possible to trace this parcel?'

'We're attending to that,' said Ransom. 'You can't give me any more information, then?'

'No, I'm sorry,' said Macintyre. 'Both these people were, as I have said, only the merest acquaintances. I met them twice in America, and so far as their private lives are concerned, I know absolutely nothing at all.'

Ransom was forced to accept this statement and took his leave. Going back to the police station, he found that the local inspector had started inquiries for the messenger who had delivered the parcel, and shortly before midnight they bore fruit.

The manager of a messenger office at Charing Cross remembered a parcel being brought in for delivery to the Chatterton, and by good luck the messenger who had taken it was on the premises. Twenty minutes later, he was in the divisional inspector's office at the police station — a rather frightened youth whose excitement at finding himself in such an important position did not outweigh his fear of anything connected with the law. His information was of the slightest. The parcel had been given to him in the course of his duties and he had delivered it to the attendant at the

Chatterton, had received a signed receipt, and had gone back to the office at Charing Cross to await fresh instructions.

The manager, interviewed later, was able to add very little to what the police already knew. The parcel had been brought into the office round about half-past six by a shabbily dressed youth of eighteen or so. He had paid the usual fee and taken his departure. The manager could give the vaguest description of this individual at first, but closer questioning resulted in his dragging up from the depths of his memory the fact that he had a finger missing on his right hand.

Ransom heard this with satisfaction. 'We ought to be able to trace him through that,' he said, and his hope was not unjustified.

At ten o'clock the next morning, a loose-limbed shifty-eyed youth was brought to Scotland Yard protesting vehemently against the injustice of the police.

'What have I done?' he demanded. 'I ain't done nothin' wrong. I try to earn an honest shillin' an' the bloomin' rozzers pinch me. What you got against me?'

'We've got nothing against you,' said Ransom soothingly. 'All we want to know is who gave you that parcel that you took to the messenger office at Charing Cross.'

The boy eyed him suspiciously. 'What was wrong with it? I took it, didn't I?'

'Yes, yes,' said the chief inspector impatiently. 'I want to know who the person was who gave it to you.'

The youth wrinkled his grimy forehead. 'She was some bird,' he remarked with a slow grin.

'She?' exclaimed Ransom. 'Was it a lady?'

'You bet your life!' said the youth with an unpleasant leer. 'The prettiest bit of goods I've seen outside the pictures. She stopped me in Villiers Street and asked me if I'd like to earn a bob. 'Take this to the messenger office at Charing Cross,' she says. 'It'll be 'alf a crown, an' 'ere's a shillin' for yourself.''

Ransom had expected anything but this. A woman! 'Who on earth could she be?' he muttered, speaking his thoughts aloud.

'I can tell you that, too,' said the youth surprisingly.

'She mentioned her name?' exclaimed

the chief inspector.

The other nodded. 'Yus! As I was leavin' 'er she said, 'In case they want to know who the sender is you can tell 'em it's Miss Catherine Lee.''

18

The Nose

The lanky youth, who rejoiced in the unpleasant name of Tom Biles, was detained
pending further inquiries. He went to the
cells in Cannon Row protesting vehemently,
and a man was sent to the address he had
given to inquire into his antecedents. These
proved to be dubious. He lived with his
mother in a narrow, dirty street off Lam-
beth Walk. The father was serving a term
of seven years' imprisonment in Worm-
wood Scrubs for 'breaking and entering
and assaulting a policeman'.

'He may be speaking the truth,' said
Ransom, 'but I doubt it. Lying comes
naturally to these fellows. We'll follow up
his story, anyway.'

A detective was dispatched to Catherine Lee's lodgings, the address of which
Ransom had obtained from Terry Ward,
and found her just as she was preparing

to leave the house to go to her work. The officer accompanied her, putting his questions as they walked along. His report when he returned to the Yard was satisfactory, so far as she was concerned.

'She knows nothing about it,' he said. 'She wasn't in the vicinity of Villiers Street last night, and couldn't have been. It was after half-past six when she left Macintyre and Sloan's, and I've checked up her movements from that time.'

'I never supposed for a moment that she did have anything to do with it,' said the inspector. 'Biles is either lying about the whole thing, or somebody's trying to frame her.'

He had more than a suspicion who that someone was, though the object of involving the woman baffled him. If Macintyre had been responsible for the sending of that box to the Renfrews, and Ransom was pretty certain on this point, he couldn't for the life of him see why the man should have tried to implicate Catherine, since it could only have the effect of indirectly leading the inquiry back to him.

There was a conference at the Yard that

morning concerning the River Men, which Terry Ward attended, and after the discussion Ransom called the young inspector into his office. Terry listened with a gloomy face to what he had to say.

'You can take it from me, sir,' he said when the chief inspector had finished, 'that Miss Lee had nothing to do with it. So far as Macintyre is concerned, I think it's more than likely that he was responsible for the deaths of the two people. I've suspected him for a long time of being behind the activities of the River Men.'

'I know you have,' said Ransom. 'The question is, how are we going to prove it? The man's clever, there's no doubt about that, and although he knows we suspect him, he also knows that we've got no evidence, and he's taking mighty good care that we shan't have any.'

'He's still under observation, I suppose?' said Terry, and Ransom nodded.

'Yes,' he said. 'From now on he'll be watched closely. That's the only hope we have of getting him. If he's concerned with these river robbers, he must communicate with them in some way, and I'm hoping we shall catch him out on that. Have you succeeded in getting anything out of those fellows you pinched at Moxon's?'

'Not a thing! They've been questioned and questioned, but they're as dumb as oysters. The whole trouble is they're more frightened of the man they are working for than they are of us. They'd rather accept their sentences philosophically and go to prison than squeal and risk the result.'

He went back to Wapping irritable and dissatisfied. The assistant commissioner who had presided at the conference had not been in an amiable mood. His remarks concerning the river police's ineffectual endeavours to apprehend the River Men had been more forcible than polite, and Terry, who knew that every effort had been made, was still feeling a little sore.

Reaching the headquarters of the Thames Police, he found a little wizened man waiting to interview him. 'Hello, Snitch!' he greeted. 'What's brought you here in the light of day?'

Snitch Keller gave his customary sniff before replying. He was a small sallow-faced man with lank black hair and weak eyes, and the chronic catarrh from which he suffered had given him his nickname. From Rotherhithe to Woolwich he was a familiar figure on the river, and the means by which he picked up a livelihood were many and varied. His chief source of income, though few suspected this — luckily for Mr. Keller — came in the form of payment for stray pieces of information which he supplied on occasion to the police. It had been through Snitch Keller that the brothers Hyman had been eventually caught, and many a river rat working out his sentence wondered spitefully during the long hours when the lock was on who had been the snout who had given him away.

'I got somethin' to tell you, Mr. Ward,' snuffled Snitch. 'Somethin' important.'

'Come into my office,' said Terry, and he led the way to his little room.

The Nose followed, and when the door was shut: 'I got the goods!' He looked round uneasily, from sheer force of habit, for there was no possibility of their being overheard. 'I've got the lowdown on these river thieves.'

Terry looked at him sharply. 'You mean the River Men?' he asked quickly.

'Yes. It ought to be worth a good bit, Mr. Ward.'

'If your information is correct,' said Terry curtly, 'you'll be suitably rewarded. What do you know about them?'

'Well, it's like this.' Snitch Keller leaned forward. 'You know Gallows Wharf?'

Terry nodded.

'Well,' continued the Nose, 'that's where the feller comes to give his orders.'

'What fellow?' asked the young inspector.

'The big feller — the boss,' said Keller impatiently. 'Twice a week 'e comes, in the early hours of the morning, an' meets the men who carry his instructions to the others.'

'Are you certain of this?' demanded Terry, his eyes sparkling.

''Ave you ever known me tell yer anythin' that wasn't right?' said Keller aggrievedly. 'You can take it as gospel,

Mr. Ward. Wednesdays and Saturdays is the days.'

Terry glanced at the calendar and made a note on a pad in front of him.

'Who's the man?' he asked.

'I don' know who 'e is. 'E's an old man with a yeller wrinkled face and a protrudin' chin. That's all I can tell yer. If you get your men to surround the place next Saturday, just before three o'clock in the mornin' you'll get 'im, then you can find out who 'e is for yourself.'

Terry stared thoughtfully in front of him. That Keller's information was correct he never doubted. He had known the little Nose for years, and never once had he let him down, and the news he had brought was of the first importance. The man in control of the River Men had always been the person Terry had wanted. Once they had got hold of him, the organization would die a natural death. He looked at the unpleasant figure of the man before him.

'You've done well, Snitch,' he said. 'We'll act on this next Saturday.'

The Nose took his departure, and

when he had gone, Terry picked up the telephone and got through to Scotland Yard. Chief Inspector Ransom listened to what he had to say and expressed his own views.

'I'll send down reinforcements,' he said. 'We'll make a good job of it on Saturday.'

Terry hung up the receiver, feeling more cheerful than he had been for days past.

19

The Leeman Corporation

Mr. Steve Copping came into Joe Hickman's Billiards Saloon shortly after that establishment had opened its doors, and with a nod to Sam, passed on to the office of the massive proprietor. Mr. Hickman was sitting gloomily at his desk, his enormous chin sunk on his broad chest, staring apparently at nothing. He looked up as Copping came in, and there was a worried expression in his small eyes.

''Morning, Joe,' said Mr. Copping. 'Any news?'

'Nothin' fresh,' Hickman said. 'I'm worried, Steve, about them fellers they took at Moxon's the other night.'

Copping shrugged his shoulders. 'Why worry about them? They won't squeal.'

'Maybe they won't, but maybe they will. You can't trust these little runts, and if they do, it's going to be mighty awkward for us.'

The genial expression on Mr. Copping's face faded and a look of uneasiness took its place. 'I shouldn't think they'd blab,' he said, but there was no conviction in his voice. 'What's put this idea into your head, Joe?'

'I've just been thinking. It won't hurt the big fellow if they do — it's us who'll get the kick, I've told you that before. Supposing one of these fellows gets windy and talks, though? How long do you think it'll be before we're in jug?' He snapped his fingers. 'As quick as that!'

Mr. Copping by now was seriously alarmed. 'What's your idea?' he asked.

Hickman made a grimace. 'I ain't got any ideas. I'm only lookin' at possibilities. We can't do nothin' now, except hope that those chaps 'ull keep their mouths shut.'

'It looks to me,' muttered Copping, 'as if we ought to think about gettin' out, Joe. We've made a tidy bit and we've been lucky, an' it's silly to go on until the luck turns.'

Mr. Hickman looked at him in silence. 'The same idea occurred to me,' he admitted. 'In fact, I've already made arrangements to sell this place.' He waved his big hand vaguely in the air. 'I've got a feller comin' in this afternoon to make an offer for the whole concern, lock, stock and barrel.'

'Have you told him?' said Copping.

'I ain't told nobody but you, and I don't intend to. The less anybody knows about it, the better. I've got all my arrangements made, and I advise you to make yours. I suppose you've got your money 'andy?'

'You bet I 'ave,' answered Copping complacently. 'I've always been prepared for somethin' like this.'

'It was bound to 'appen,' declared Mr. Hickman. 'It don't matter 'ow clever a feller is, or 'ow carefully 'e lays 'is plans, somethin's bound to go wrong sooner or later, and that business at Moxon's was *it*.'

'When are you thinkin' of quittin'?'

'As soon as possible. I don't mind tellin' you, Steve, I've seen the red light and I'm gettin' out before it flares up into a blaze. You can take it from me this ramp ain't goin' to last much longer. The police ain't fools, and they always win in the long run. The wise feller is the feller who gets out before the smash comes, and I reckon I'm goin' to be wise.'

Mr. Copping nodded in agreement. 'I'm with you, Joe. There's a lot of sense in what you say. We'd better not do anythin' until after Saturday, though. He's got another coup planned, and there's bags of dough in it. We might as well have that before we quit.'

A little greedy glitter came into the small eyes of the man before him. 'I suppose we might,' he said, 'but it's a risk. It's these fellers I'm afraid of, Steve; if they talk we're for it, an' you never know when they're going to.'

'They haven't yet. If they 'ad, we shouldn't be sittin' 'ere.'

The big man was not so sure of this, and said so. 'You can never tell what these busies are up to. They're as cunnin' as monkeys; they may be just playin' with us, watchin' us in the hope that they'll learn something that'll give 'em a line to the Big Feller. I'm all for goin' while the goin's good.'

He got up laboriously, moved to the door and peered out. There were only half a dozen men in the billiard hall, four playing a desultory game of snooker and the other two looking on. Coming back, he closed the door and dropped his voice.

'See here, Steve,' he said in a hoarse whisper, 'I've known you for some time an' I can trust you. These are my plans.' He spoke rapidly in so low a tone that Mr. Copping had to strain his ears to hear what he said. When he had finished, he nodded.

'You can count me in, Joe,' he said, and held out his hand. 'Now I must go; I've got to see Mills.'

He left Mr. Hickman, a thoughtful and very worried man, but his worry was to some extent counterbalanced by the suggestion his friend had put forward.

A bus carried him to Limehouse, and making his way through a maze of narrow streets, he eventually came to the entrance to a medium-sized warehouse that stood on the riverbank. On the weather-stained gates had been painted in letters of startling newness the words 'Leeman Corporation'. There was nothing to signify what business the Leeman Corporation transacted, but moored to the long wharfage were two decrepit tugs and a number of barges, which seemed to suggest that they were lightermen.

Mr. Copping was evidently familiar with the place, for he found his way without difficulty to a small and dingy office facing the river, in which a thin unpleasant-looking man was engaged in making entries in a greasy ledger. Mr. Copping spoke quickly to him, and the man interspersed his remarks with brief nods of his narrow head.

The Leeman Corporation was a perfectly legitimate business which had come into being eight months previously. That is to say, it was legitimate so far as the business which it conducted appeared on the books. There was another side to its activities of which few people were aware, and this was by far the most profitable.

The contracts which the Leeman

Corporation undertook were few and far between, for their tugs were old and out of date, and their charges excessive in comparison with other firms of a similar nature. Nobody had ever seen the head of the firm, for Mr. Leeman controlled his business by telephone, and the manager was the only person in authority who ever passed the gates.

'You'll attend to that, Mills?' said Mr. Copping, and the thin-faced Mills nodded. He was a man of few words, taciturn and abrupt.

'Pity about that Moxon business,' he said. 'It would have been a good haul.'

Mr. Copping nodded. 'Can't be lucky all the time, and we haven't done so badly.'

Mills agreed.

'Got rid of that last lot?' asked Copping.

'Went yesterday. A consignment of timber to Gravesend.'

Steve Copping grinned. 'There was nothing woody about them cigars,' he remarked. 'Got much on the premises?'

'Very little now,' Mills said, for the real business of the Leeman Corporation was to act as cover and dispose of the loot acquired by the activities of the River Men. To this warehouse, concealed in innocent-looking coal and timber barges, came the results of the various warehouse raids; and Terry Ward, if he could have examined some of the barges which the Leeman Corporation's wheezy tugs towed slowly up- and downriver, would have found an answer to his most puzzling problem — the means by which the River Men succeeded in getting the proceeds of their robberies away.

In every instance where a robbery had taken place, a barge belonging to the Leeman Corporation, loaded with coal or timber, had been moored close to the warehouse which had been broken into, and a careful examination would have revealed that below the heaped coal or carefully stacked wood was a space in which the River Men had concealed the stolen property. In nearly every case, when the police had been examining the premises and puzzling their brains to discover how the stolen stuff had been removed, it was within a few yards of them, hidden in the dingy barge which lay moored to the wharf. The organization necessary to ensure this had been tremendous, but the unknown who had devised scheme was a genius at organization; and having marked down the warehouse which was to suffer next, he had sometimes waited weeks until it could be arranged that a Leeman Corporation barge could, without suspicion, be brought to the vicinity. The barges were specially constructed; and the entrance, giving admission to the concealed chamber beneath the cargo, was cleverly hidden.

Mr. Copping completed his business, and was preparing to take his leave when the telephone rang, and Mills took off the receiver of the old instrument.

'Hello!' he growled, and then his voice changed. 'Oh, it's you, sir, is it?'

He listened to the message that came over the wire and then: 'He's here now, as a matter of fact; would you like to speak to him?' The reply must have been in the affirmative, for he turned to Mr. Copping. 'The guv'nor's on the telephone,' he said, 'and wants to speak to you.'

Copping took the receiver from his

hand and held it to his ear, and the familiar harsh voice of the old man reached him.

'Listen, Copping,' it said. 'I've got some fresh instructions for you. Listen carefully, and make sure there's no mistake.'

Mr. Copping listened carefully for the next ten minutes.

'Is that clear?' said the voice, when the man at the other end of the wire had finished.

'Sure!' said Copping. 'But why — '

'Never mind why, just do as I say!' snapped the other, 'and don't make any mistake. It's important. And you've no need to say anything to Mills; it's not his business.'

He rang off, and Copping hung up the receiver with a frown.

'What did he have to say?' asked Mills curiously.

'Nothing concerning you,' answered Copping. 'He wants me to do something for him, that's all.'

He left the premises of the Leeman Corporation shortly after, turning over the orders that the unknown had given him in his mind, and he was rather puzzled to know why they had been issued.

He walked as far as Poplar, found a post office, and entering bought a letter-card. Carrying it over to the counter from which wires could be sent, he wrote slowly and laboriously with long pauses for thought. When he had finished, he sealed the card, addressed it, and leaving the post office, slipped it into the box. He had carried out the first part of his instructions, and made his way back to Joe Hickman's in order to discuss his own and that gentleman's immediate future.

20

Under Cover of Darkness

The letter which Mr. Copping had posted in Poplar arrived at Messrs. Macintyre and Sloan's by the afternoon post. Catherine Lee eyed the uneducated hand, saw that the epistle bore the word 'personal' heavily underlined in one corner, and carried it into the inner office.

Macintyre received it with a grunt. He was poring over a letter which had come that morning bearing the Belgian postmark, decoding the contents with the aid of a small red-covered notebook which lay on his desk. He covered both up quickly as Catherine came in, but not quickly enough to prevent her seeing that the letter was similar to the one he had received before.

She went back to her own room and sat down at her desk, her face puckered into a thoughtful frown. For some minutes she sat idly staring at the typewriter in front of her. Eventually she came to a decision, for presently her face cleared and she continued her work briskly. At six o'clock, Macintyre's bell rang and she answered the summons. He was standing by his desk, his hat and coat on, apparently on the point of departure. There was no sign of the letter or the little red book, Catherine noted, and waited to receive his instructions.

'You were at the Chatterton the other night, Miss Lee,' he began abruptly.

'Yes, I was, Mr. Macintyre.'

'And I believe the police have been questioning you concerning the parcel that was delivered to those unfortunate people who were killed?'

She nodded again, wondering how he had become aware of this.

'Did they say anything about me?'

'No, they never mentioned you, Mr. Macintyre.'

'Hm! That's all I wanted to know,' he snapped curtly, and jerked his head towards the inner door, his usual sign of dismissal.

She went back to her own room and began to tidy up her desk before leaving, wondering why he had bothered to call her in for such a trivial inquiry. There were other and more important matters occupying her mind, however, and she dismissed this minor problem to give her whole attention to them.

She took a circuitous route to her lodgings, passing through a nearby shopping centre, and at an ironmonger's made a peculiar purchase. With this wrapped up in paper beneath her arm, she went home. By the time she had washed, her frugal dinner was ready and she ate it slowly, reading the evening paper which she had brought in with her.

When the meal was finished, she occupied herself with one or two domestic trifles that had to be attended to, and then settled down to pass the remainder of the evening with a book.

It is doubtful if she could have remembered what the story was about, for her mind was very active, but she forced herself to concentrate more or less on the printed pages to calm the excitement which had taken possession of her.

At twelve o'clock, she laid the book aside and began her preparations for the night. Going to the cupboard which served as a wardrobe, she took out a tweed skirt and a pair of flat-heeled brogues. These she put on, completing her toilet by pulling a beret over her hair. In the pocket of a dark raincoat she put her purchase from the ironmonger's and an electric torch, and slipping the coat on opened the door of her room and listened.

The household were working people who rose early and had long since been in bed. Softly and stealthily, without making a sound, she crept out into the passage, closed her door, and began to make her way down the narrow staircase. With steady fingers, she unfastened the chain and pulled back the bolt that secured the front door, slipped across the threshold and drew it to softly behind her.

It was a fine night but dark, and she walked swiftly along the deserted streets towards her objective. It was one o'clock when she came into Butcher Road and paused near the dark bulk of the offices that housed the activities of Messrs. Macintyre and Sloan. The main gates were closed and locked, and passing them she turned into a narrow passageway that ran down to the river, came out on to the wharfage, and searched in the darkness for the little boat which she knew was moored at this point.

She located it and began to climb down the crazy ladder that led to a small landing-stage. Stepping from this into the boat, she untied the painter, and paddling with one oar, sent the dinghy gently along the frontage until it bumped softly against the moored barge that was tied up to the wharf. To this she made the boat fast and with difficulty succeeded in scrambling aboard. She had to jump the three feet that separated the deck of the barge from the wharf, and she succeeded in accomplishing this without mishap.

The worst part of her task was over. Picking her way among the debris that strewed the frontage, she stopped by a narrow door that gave admittance to the warehouse. This, she knew, was locked, but from the pocket of her raincoat she took a key, and a second later had opened the door and passed into the darkness beyond.

There was no night watchman kept at Macintyre and Sloan's, and when the door had closed behind her, she breathed more easily. The light of her torch cut through the darkness, and swiftly she made her way across the lower floor to the staircase which led to the offices above. She opened the door of her own room, passed in, and with another key unlocked the door which communicated with Macintyre's private office.

Her heart was beating with excitement as she stood in the familiar shadowy room. So far everything had gone without a hitch. Another hour at the most, and she would have finished what she had come to do and be on her way home. She put her torch down on a chair, directing its light so that it fell on the desk, and taking from her pocket the chisel which she had bought earlier that evening, went over and examined the drawers. They were all locked as she had expected, but the chisel made short work of the flimsy fastening, and she soon had the first one open.

Hurriedly but methodically, she searched the contents. What she had come to find was not here. She tried the next drawer, but there was no need to do more than glance in this, for it contained nothing but printed stationery. The third drawer occupied her attention without result, and she paused for a moment before tackling the others. There was a possibility that her search would be unsuccessful. It was not unlikely, indeed probable, that Macintyre would have taken the thing she wanted home with him. It was only a chance that he would leave it in his desk, but it was a chance that had been worth trying.

She broke open the fourth drawer and drew in her breath sharply as almost the first thing she saw was the little red notebook which Macintyre used for decoding those mysterious letters from Belgium.

In the excitement of her discovery, she failed to hear the creak of the loose board in her own office, and the first warning she had that she was no longer alone was the click of the switch and a blaze of light as the lights came on.

With a gasp, she spun round towards the door. At the same instant, a voice said sharply:

'What are you doing here?'

Framed in the open doorway stood Macintyre. As she turned, he recognized her and his eyes narrowed.

'Why, it's Miss Lee!' he said, and then as he looked past her to the desk and saw the open drawers. 'So you add burglary to your other accomplishments. May I inquire what you're doing in my office at this hour of the morning?'

21

The Compact

The shock of Macintyre's sudden entrance had been severe and unexpected, and it took Catherine some seconds to recover. For a moment she could only stare at him dumbly.

The little red-covered book which she had been holding when he had surprised her had fallen from her fingers to the carpet, and his eyes travelled slowly from her face to that vivid patch of colour.

He came in, closed the door, walked over to her side, and stooping, picked up the book and slipped it into his pocket. 'Now, Miss Lee,' he said, and the expression on his face was unpleasant, 'perhaps you'll explain what you're doing here and why I shouldn't inform the police and have you arrested?'

She had recovered from her first shock by now and faced him coolly. 'It doesn't appear to me as if any explanation *was* necessary,' she said steadily. 'Surely it's obvious to the meanest intelligence why I'm here.'

He stood looking at her, his hands in his pockets. 'You take it very calmly,' he remarked. 'I suppose you realize what the result would be if I called a policeman?'

'Why not try it and see?' she suggested. 'Perhaps I'd have something to say to the police, too.'

His lips compressed. 'What do you mean?'

'Ask yourself that question! I've no doubt the police would be as interested to see that little book you have in your pocket as I am, and also the code letters which you've been receiving lately from Belgium.'

He frowned. 'It seems I got the wrong impression of you, Miss Lee,' he murmured. 'I was under the impression that you were just an ordinary, nice woman, quite a capable secretary, and nothing else.'

'Continue to think I'm a nice woman,' said Catherine. 'I am, but that doesn't mean I'm dumb.'

'What do you know about those Belgian letters?' he demanded.

She smiled.

'Very little,' she replied candidly. 'If you hadn't interrupted me when you did, I should probably have known a great deal more.'

He eyed her contemplatively. This woman had given him one of the greatest surprises of his life. After finishing decoding the letter, he had slipped the little code book into a drawer of his desk and had forgotten all about it until he had reached home. Later that evening, he had discovered that it was necessary for the business he was attending to, and remembered where he had put it. A taxi had brought him to Butcher Road, he had let himself in, and ascending the stairs to his office, had heard the noise Catherine made in forcing the drawers. He had concluded that he would find a very ordinary burglar at work, and his astonishment when he discovered who the night intruder was had been little less than Catherine's own. And now, instead of tears and protestations, he was faced with this cool business-like attitude which rather disconcerted him.

'How long have you been a burglar and potential blackmailer?' he asked.

She shrugged her shoulders. 'This is the first time. The truth of the matter is, Mr. Macintyre, my salary is so small and my tastes are so expensive that it's necessary I should find some means of augmenting my income.'

'And you expect to augment it from me?' he said.

'I live in hope,' she replied brightly. 'After all, you're quite well off; and you don't want any trouble, do you?'

'You're an extraordinary woman!' he muttered, pulling out his cigarette-case. 'Really, you interest me enormously.'

'Am I to take that as a compliment?' she said, and when he made no reply, occupying himself with lighting a cigarette: 'I'll have one of those, too, if you don't mind. I've forgotten mine, and burglary is rather trying to the nerves.'

He held out his case without a word and she helped herself calmly.

'What did you expect to find?' he said after they had smoked in silence for some time. 'What brought you here?'

'Curiosity,' she answered. 'I wanted to know the contents of those letters, and I thought perhaps at the same time there might be one or two things of value that I could pick up.'

'Amazing!' he murmured. 'Well, you're certainly candid about it, anyway. D'you know, I think, Miss Lee, that it's perhaps very lucky that I came tonight as I did.'

'I hope it turns out to be!'

'It seems to me,' he continued thoughtfully, 'that you might be very useful.'

She flicked the ash from her cigarette. 'I *am* very useful. I'm an excellent secretary and a most efficient book-keeper, for which I receive a salary that's scarcely sufficient to keep a roof over my head.'

'I didn't exactly mean in that capacity,' he answered, and his cold eyes surveyed her appraisingly.

'I'm open to any suggestions,' she said. 'I'm not bad to look at, and I have brains. I should be an asset to anyone who's prepared to make it worth my while.'

'I believe you would.'

'Neither am I stupidly conventional. The law is a very fine thing so long as it provides protection for people against the depredations of thieves and others. But when it stands in the way of making a comfortable living — well, I'm quite open to conviction.'

He stared at her. Until now, he had regarded this woman whom he had seen every day for the past eight months merely as part of Macintyre and Sloan's; the same as he looked upon the office furniture. He had never imagined that she was anything else but an ordinary hard-working secretary who performed her duties satisfactorily and drew her pay envelope every Friday. But this evening had revealed her as something very different, something that he was not quite sure how to deal with. The vague threat she had uttered when he had suggested calling the police was a source of uneasiness. He had no idea how much she knew or guessed. She had been in a position to learn a lot, and it was better that they should come to an amicable understanding than that he should risk his plans being ruined by a precipitant action.

'I believe it was providential that I happened to come back to the office tonight,' he said. 'I think, Miss Lee, that I can put something in your way that will be very profitable.'

'That sounds good to me,' she said. 'What is it?'

'I can't tell you here and now. The hour is late and I have a taxi waiting to take me back to the West End. Suppose we have a talk tomorrow?'

She nodded. 'When?'

'I shall be a little late in the morning,' he said, 'and there's the foreign mail to attend to. Suppose we have our chat in the afternoon?'

'That suits me,' she replied, and rose from where she had been sitting on the edge of the desk. 'Perhaps it would be as well if I came with you as far as the street. It'll save me a lot of trouble. It's not very easy climbing over barges in the dark.'

He smiled grimly. 'So that's the way you got in?'

'That's the way. I took an impression of

the key to the storeroom door some weeks ago and had one cut.'

He eyed her admiringly. 'You certainly are the coolest person I've ever come across.'

'I'm not only the coolest,' she remarked, 'but I'm the coldest! It's a pity they never installed central heating in this place.'

He laughed, and switching out the lights, preceded her through her little office to the stairway. Outside the entrance to the warehouse, a taxi was waiting.

'Can I drop you anywhere?' he suggested.

'No, thank you,' she answered dryly. 'I may be a burglar, but I draw the line at riding alone with men in taxis late at night. Good night, Mr. Macintyre, and don't forget tomorrow afternoon.'

He watched her as she hurried away up the street, and then giving the address of his flat, got into the taxi and was driven off.

From a narrow turning where it had stood concealed a second cab emerged and began to follow the first, keeping at a respectful distance behind. Looking back through the little window, Macintyre saw the pursuing lights and smiled grimly. He knew that he was being trailed, and wondered what the watcher would think of his reappearance accompanied by Catherine Lee from the closed and locked warehouse. It would be something, at any rate, for his superiors at Scotland Yard to puzzle their brains over when he made his report.

22

The Night of the Raid

The morning of Saturday was dull and grey. Although not actually raining, the leaden clouds which obscured the sky hinted that rain was not very far off.

Terry Ward woke early, with a feeling of expectancy. Tonight, with a bit of luck, would see the end of his long and dreary search and the capture of the man who controlled the nefarious destinies of the River Men. His mind was full of his forthcoming plans as he shaved and dressed. A further conference with Ransom had resulted in a complete and comprehensive plan of campaign. Terry and his men would look after the river end, Ransom and the Flying Squad would take charge of all land entries to Gallows Wharf.

Thirty men had been picked for the job, and there seemed no possibility that, providing the unknown came at all, he could elude their vigilance.

Terry had seen nothing of Snitch Keller since he had crept into Wapping Station to unfold his startling information, but this was not unusual. On previous occasions, the little Nose had delivered his message and made himself scarce. He had, as Terry knew very well, no wish to be mixed up in the subsequent results of his betrayal, for there were men on the river who would have dealt very hardly with him had they been aware of his occupation. Indeed, it was surprising that Snitch had managed to carry on for so long. Whenever news came through that a body had been taken from the Thames, Terry expected to hear that the informer had reached the end of his life of spying, but in some extraordinary way Keller continued to poke and pry without being suspected.

Terry spent the morning at his headquarters at Wapping dealing with the ordinary routine work, and at one o'clock went up to Scotland Yard for an interview with Ransom to fix the final details of the arrangements for the night. The chief inspector had a large map of Greenwich Reach and the surrounding districts spread out on his desk before him. He looked up as Terry came in.

'Pull that chair up, Ward,' he said. 'Before we go into the matter of this business tonight, I've got a peculiar piece of information for you.'

Terry raised his eyebrows. 'What's that?'

'It concerns that woman, Catherine Lee,' said Ransom. 'I'm not so sure she isn't mixed up in the business somehow, after all.' He paused, and Terry waited, wondering what was coming next. 'You know we've had Macintyre under observation for several days? Well, the night before last, the man who was trailing him followed him to Macintyre and Sloan's. He chose a peculiar time for going there, half-past one in the morning, and he drove from his flat in a taxi. Burridge followed in another, saw him let himself into the warehouse, and waited, wondering what the idea was that took him to the place at that time of the morning. Macintyre kept his cab waiting, and was in the building altogether about half an hour. Our man had left his own taxi round the corner, and presently he saw Macintyre come out, accompanied by Miss Lee.'

Terry uttered an exclamation. 'He must have been mistaken!' he said incredulously.

'I don't think he was. He gave me a pretty good description of the woman he saw, and there's very little doubt that it was Miss Lee. She went off up the street, and Macintyre got into his cab and was driven home. Now the question is, what was she doing at such an unusual hour?'

'Maybe it was some business connected with the firm.'

The chief inspector gave him a sceptical look. 'At one-thirty in the morning?' he asked ironically. 'No, I don't think that explanation's any good. It looks to me more likely that Macintyre had arranged a meeting with her that he didn't want anyone to know about, and I'm wondering if perhaps, after all, she wasn't in that business at the Chatterton.'

'I'm sure she wasn't!' declared Terry.

'I'd be willing to stake my life Miss Lee's straight!'

'Hm!' said Ransom noncommittally. 'Well, you must admit it's peculiar all the same. Private secretaries of commercial firms don't usually do business at half-past one in the morning with their employers — not at the business premises, anyway.'

'There must be some explanation — ' began Terry, but the chief inspector interrupted him.

'Of course there's an explanation,' he said. 'The question is — what is it? Why did she go to Macintyre and Sloan's to meet Macintyre at that hour?'

Terry was silent, his forehead wrinkled. He could offer no feasible explanation. It was extraordinary! He was not surprised that Ransom was suspicious.

'There's nothing against the law in it,' he said feebly.

'I agree with you. But it's one of those things that require explaining, and when a thing requires explaining you can bet your life there's something wrong about it.' He changed the subject abruptly. 'We've cabled to America asking for all the information they can give us concerning Renfrew and his wife. And also anything that was known about Macintyre during the time he was out there. Maybe their reply will make interesting reading.'

He picked up a pencil. 'Now, about tonight,' he said, and Terry, trying vainly to wipe Catherine Lee from his mind, drew up his chair. 'Here's Gallows Wharf,' continued Ransom, and he drew a circle on the map. 'The main entrance is in Thames Street, and it's one of those crazy buildings that project out over the river and are supported on piles.'

Terry nodded. 'I know it well.'

'I've had a man exploring the vicinity all day yesterday. If we plant our fellows in Thames Street, we block all means of escape that way. There are two narrow alleys leading out of Thames Street down to the river, and they can be closed. Now, if you can bring your men up to the Middlesex shore here and here — ' He made two swift crosses on the map with his pencil. ' — you can cover anybody who tries to leave by water. My men have

251

instructions not to interfere with anyone entering the building, but they're to pull in any man, woman, or child who attempts to leave; you'd better instruct your fellows to do the same. Did Keller say how this man comes?'

'No; he only said he gets there round about three.'

'Well, it's occurred to me,' said Ransom, 'that he may come by river. You'd better be prepared for that, as it's your department. I should suggest that you arrange for all launches to run without lights, and tell them to take up their positions by midnight, keeping hidden as much as possible. My men will arrive at Thames Street just before twelve, and if we see anybody go in, we shall force an entrance. As we arranged, the signal will be a rocket, with red and white stars. We'll keep a lookout for that, and you keep a lookout too. If the man comes by river, you signal; if he comes by land, we signal. Is that clear?'

It was so clear that a child could have understood it. Terry said so.

'Then that's all, I think,' remarked

Ransom. 'We can only wait and see what happens.'

Terry left him to go back to Wapping and make his preparations for the night, but his mind was chiefly concerned with the piece of news he had learnt regarding Catherine Lee, and throughout the rest of the day he worried about her. He was to worry more before very long, but luckily the future was mercifully hidden from him.

23

The Man Who Came

The threat of rain which had hung about all day was fulfilled at seven o'clock, when it began to pour in torrents. The streets and gutters ran with water, and by ten there was no sign of the storm abating.

'Looks as if we're going to have a pleasant night,' grunted a weather-beaten sergeant to Terry as they stood under cover at Wapping Station and watched the downpour.

'A little rain won't hurt you,' said the young inspector. 'Is everything ready?'

'Yes, sir. Three launches trimmed up and waiting.'

'Then you'd better go and have some hot coffee or something. It'll warm you up.'

Twenty of the river police had been ordered for this duty, and were grouped in the common-room drinking hot coffee made by the night orderly.

Terry sought out the officers who were to be in charge of the other two boats and made certain that their instructions were clear.

'If we see anyone come by river,' he said, 'we fire a rocket to warn the land men. They'll do the same should the man we're expecting come by road. One boat load will cross to the Surrey shore and effect an entrance to the warehouse from the wharf. Any strangers, no matter who they are, found on the premises are to be arrested.'

It was a quarter to eleven when they left in the police boat and began to make their way downstream through the falling rain. All lights that identified them as belonging to the river police had been removed from the launches — a precaution that was rendered necessary in case the man they were hoping to take should become aware of their presence.

The night was very dark and the falling rain made visibility difficult. Terry, in charge of the first boat, stood by the man at the helm and peered into the wet blackness. The river was quiet. Here and there a flare on the shore marked the spot where men were working, loading or unloading at one of the wharves. But for the most part, work had ceased for the day. The gurgle of the water round the bows and the hiss of the rain kept a running accompaniment to the soft chug-chug of the powerful engine.

'Make for that line of barges,' said Terry as they came within sight of Gallows Wharf.

The engineer-steersman nodded and sent his boat towards the Middlesex shore. A line of moored barges offered a good cover here, and the police boat slowly nosed its way in among them and was brought skilfully to rest under the shadow of a big coal barge. The other two boats, following Terry's lead, crept into position, and taking a pair of night glasses from the pocket of his oilskins, Terry scanned the face of Gallows Wharf. The rotting structure rose into the night scarcely discernible in the darkness, but there was no sign of life.

The young inspector had not expected

there would be. It was early yet, barely twelve, and the time for the unknown to make his appearance according to Snitch Keller was three. If he kept to this timetable, they had nearly three hours' wait ahead of them. It had been Ransom's suggestion that they should take up their positions in good time in order that any watcher who might be sent ahead to spy out the land should see nothing unusual.

Terry settled down for the long wait. Every light on board the launches had been extinguished, and they had been manoeuvred into positions where it was impossible they could be seen from anyone on the river.

The rain continued to fall unceasingly. A cargo boat passed them once, moving slowly downstream from the direction of the Pool, followed later by a tug towing an empty barge; but apart from these, there was little or no traffic.

The time passed slowly. To Terry, whose nerves were keyed up, it seemed to almost stand still. Again and again he glanced at the luminous watch on his wrist, and once he held it to his ear under the impression that it had stopped, but the steady ticking reassured him.

It was just before three that their long vigil was rewarded. Above the hiss of the rain and the faint sounds that came from the direction of the Pool, he heard the splash of oars, and levelling his glasses, swept the darkness of the river. Although he could see nothing, he knew that a rowboat was approaching. His ears told him that the person who rowed was not a skilled waterman; the dip of the oars was uneven, and every now and again there was a splash as the rower made a false stroke.

Presently, a scarcely discernible blot of darkness against the blackness of the water, he saw the boat. It looked like a small dinghy, and it was moving slowly downstream. As it drew nearer, it was possible to make out vaguely the form of the rower seated amidships. It came nearer, nearer, turned towards the forest of piles that supported the overhung front of the deserted warehouse, and was brought to rest amidst them.

Sounds carry clearly on the river, and Terry was able to hear the dull thuds the rower made as he shipped his oars. He could see nothing now of the boat or its occupant, for it had disappeared in the dense shadow thrown by the overhanging structure, but he knew that it had been moored somewhere amidst the numerous supporting piles.

'That's our man,' he whispered to his sergeant. 'There must be some way into the warehouse from there. We'll wait a minute or two so as to give him time to get well inside, and then we'll fire the rocket.'

He allowed three minutes to elapse and then snapped his fingers. The river policeman who had been waiting for the signal struck a match and applied it to the touch-paper of the rocket which had been mounted near the small cabin. There was a hissing roar, and amid a shower of golden sparks, the rocket soared into the black sky. It exploded in a burst of red and white stars which fell slowly towards the river.

'Now!' said Terry to the man in charge

of the launch, and he started the engine.

The boat moved forward, took a wide sweep, and came upstream on the Surrey side. Slowing as it neared Gallows Wharf, it drifted up to the piles, and leaning over the gunwale, Terry grasped one of the slimy supports. He could see the empty rowboat in which the unknown had come and also the end of the rope ladder that dangled into it.

As he prepared to scramble from the launch to the boat, he heard the sound of echoing blows and guessed that Ransom and his men were breaking into the place from the front. Pulling an automatic from his pocket, he thumbed back the safety catch and began to ascend the ladder. He had seen the square opening above and guessed that it was a trap leading into the warehouse. He scrambled through into pitch darkness, and had barely risen to his feet when somebody cannoned into him. He heard a muttered oath and grasped an arm. It was wrenched from his hand, and a heavy blow caught him on the chin. It made him stagger, but he kept his balance and launched himself in the direction of the heavy breathing which told him the position of his assailant.

The other overbalanced under the force of his spring and they both crashed heavily to the floor. Terry's pistol flew from his hand, and then strong fingers gripped his throat. He tried to free himself, but the strangling grasp grew tighter. His adversary seemed to possess abnormal strength, and nothing he could do succeeded in shifting that merciless hold.

He felt his senses reeling. Vaguely, as from a long way off, he heard shouts ... Lights flashed in the big, shadowy warehouse and the place became full of men ...

Just as he felt that he must breathe or die, the fingers were torn from his throat and he lay back gasping, drawing great panting gulps of life-giving air into his tortured lungs. His head cleared and he staggered to his feet, his throat sore, and a little dizzy, but otherwise normal.

'Have you got him?' he gasped.

Inspector Ransom nodded grimly. 'Yes, we've got him,' he said, and jerked his head towards the man who was struggling in the grip of two burly constables. 'He's a nice specimen; I think you know him rather well.'

Terry looked into the rage-distorted face of Roy Hugh Macintyre!

24

The Thing in the Chair

'So it's you, is it?' said Terry pleasantly. 'Well, I'm not surprised. I've always suspected you were behind the River Men.'

'Well, you're wrong!' snarled Macintyre hoarsely. 'I know nothing about the River Men, and I'd like an explanation of this outrage.'

'Outrage, eh!' snapped Ransom. 'The best thing you can do, Macintyre, is to keep quiet. We'll take any statement you like to make later. In the meanwhile, if you feel like talking, explain *that*!' He pointed to something that lolled in a chair by the side of a bare-topped table. Macintyre ceased his struggles and his face went white.

'I know nothing about that,' he muttered. 'Who is he?'

Terry had gone over and was looking

down at the huddled figure. 'Snitch Keller!' he breathed in horror, and hardened as he was, he could not repress a shudder as he looked at all that remained of the little nose. Snitch had come by his death violently. He sat huddled in the chair, his head and shoulders a mass of blood, for he had died from a savage blow that had crushed the back of his skull.

'I know nothing about it, I tell you,' said Macintyre as he looked from one to the other of the accusing faces round him. 'I didn't know he was here and I've never seen him before. He was like that when I came.'

'Tell that to the judge!' said Ransom curtly. 'Perhaps he'll believe you.'

'It's the truth! As God's my judge, it's the truth! I came here tonight to keep an appointment — '

'I'll bet you did,' said Terry sternly, and he looked at the pathetic figure of the little Nose.

'No, no, not with him,' cried Macintyre. 'I tell you I've never seen him before. I came to meet — to meet somebody with whom I'm doing a bit of business — '

'At three o'clock in the morning at an empty warehouse,' broke in Chief Inspector Ransom derisively. 'You expect us to believe that, Macintyre?'

'It's the truth,' said Macintyre hoarsely.

'Who were you going to meet?' asked Terry.

'A man called Copping,' came the reply without hesitation. 'I was doing some business with him which — well, it wasn't strictly legal, and he wrote me suggesting that this would be a good place to discuss it.'

'Have you got the letter?' asked Ransom.

'No, I destroyed it. It wasn't the sort of thing I wanted to fall into other hands. I burnt it.'

'So we've nothing but your word that this man Copping did make an appointment to meet you here?' said Ransom. 'What was this business you were doing with him?'

Macintyre hesitated.

'Don't think up any lies, Macintyre,' said Ransom roughly. 'Come clean!'

'Well, it concerns — drugs,' answered

Macintyre slowly.

'You mean smuggling dangerous drugs into the country?' exclaimed the chief inspector.

'Yes. I suppose I may as well make a clean breast of it. I thought there was money in drugs, and I had arranged with Copping for a consignment of cocaine, opium, and morphia to be sent me from Belgium concealed in a cargo of bricks. The majority of the bricks were to be genuine; only a few, specially designated with a secret mark, contained the drugs. The bricks were to be brought by river and unloaded at my warehouse. The genuine bricks were going to a genuine destination, and the marked ones were to be removed and the drugs extracted. That's all. Now you know everything!'

'I suppose this was a sideline to the River Men,' said Terry, and Macintyre swung round.

'I tell you I don't know anything about the River Men!' he snapped angrily. 'I've nothing to do with them!'

'Well, that remains to be seen,' grunted Ransom. 'You're under arrest, Macintyre, and the charge at present is being found on enclosed premises with unlawful intent. There will be others later of a more serious nature, I've no doubt. Take him along to the cooler.'

Macintyre opened his lips, but whatever he was going to say remained unuttered, for he closed them again without speaking, and quietly allowed himself to be led away by the two policemen. When he had gone, Ransom turned to Terry.

'Did you ever hear such a thin story in your life?' he asked. 'Nothing to do with the River Men! I'll bet he's the fellow we're after. I don't think there's any doubt of it.'

'I don't either,' agreed Terry. 'There's only one thing that's puzzling me, Ransom. When poor little Keller came to lay his information, he said that the man who came here was an old man with a protruding chin. By no stretch of the imagination could that description apply to Macintyre.'

'Maybe he used to disguise himself,' said the chief inspector, frowning.

'Then why wasn't he disguised tonight?'

'I don't know; perhaps he didn't bother. You're not suggesting there's another man, are you?'

'No, I'm just wondering, that's all.'

'I don't think you need to! It's as plain as the sun on a summer day. Macintyre's the man we want all right, and he's hoping to get away with the lesser charge of peddling dope. But the murder of that fellow will take a lot of explaining away.' He walked over and frowned down at the body. 'He's been dead for some time,' he remarked. 'The blood's dried.'

'Which seems to let Macintyre out, for he didn't arrive until a few minutes ago.'

Ransom scratched his chin irritably. 'Are you setting up as counsel for his defence?' he inquired.

Terry smiled. 'No; I'm merely pointing out the facts.'

'Well, don't! I can see them for myself. There was nothing to prevent Macintyre meeting this fellow earlier in the evening and killing him then, was there?'

'Nothing,' said Terry, 'except that it seems rather a risky proceeding. Why leave the body here? Why not drop it into the river? Nobody but a lunatic would return to a place where he'd just committed a murder and left the body of his victim as evidence against him.'

'Crooks do funny things,' commented Ransom, but Terry could see that he was impressed by this reasoning. 'Maybe he was disturbed and couldn't complete his job. Maybe he was coming back to tip the body in the river as you suggest. Anyhow, we'll go into that later.' He turned to his sergeant. 'Send one of your men to find a doctor,' he ordered.

The sergeant passed the order on, and Ransom glanced round the gloomy apartment. 'We'd better make a search of this place,' he said, and Terry and he, with the assistance of their men, made a close inspection of the deserted warehouse from roof to cellars. They found nothing, however, to reward their diligent search except the little electric buzzer which had been fixed to the wall near the table. Tracing the wires from this, they discovered that they ran to a push screwed to the top of one of the piles below the trap.

'Obviously,' said Ransom when this

discovery was made, 'the place has been used pretty frequently. I wonder what Keller meant by an old man? It seems incredible he could have mistaken Macintyre for such a person.'

Terry grinned to himself. Evidently the chief inspector had been thinking over his remarks. 'Possibly your suggestion is the right one,' he said, 'and Macintyre used to come here in disguise.'

The doctor arrived as they completed their search and made a brief examination of the dead man. 'Whoever killed him must have been pretty powerful,' he said when he had finished. 'That blow has splintered his skull like an eggshell. I doubt if he ever knew what killed him.'

'How long do you think he's been dead?' asked Ransom.

The doctor pursed his lips. 'Difficult to say with any degree of exactitude. Certainly six or seven hours.'

The chief inspector glanced at his watch — it was then a little after half-past four. 'Which means he was killed round about nine o'clock,' he muttered. 'Hm! Perhaps the man who was keeping

Macintyre under observation will be able to tell us something.'

But his hope was doomed to disappointment, for when in the early hours of the morning Terry accompanied him back to Scotland Yard, they discovered a disconsolate police officer waiting to receive them.

'I'm very sorry, Mr. Ransom,' said Burridge, 'but I lost that feller this evening. He must have been aware that he was being followed, and he gave me the slip.'

'When was this?' asked Ransom sharply.

'Just before eight. He left his house at a quarter past seven and travelled by Tube to Blackfriars; that's where he dodged me.'

The chief inspector gave Terry a significant glance which the young inspector correctly interpreted. If Macintyre had been in the region of Blackfriars at a quarter to eight, he would have had ample time to get to Gallows Wharf and kill Keller by nine. He answered the unspoken question which he could see in Ransom's eyes.

'You're wondering how he enticed Keller into the deserted warehouse?' he said.

The chief inspector nodded. 'Right, I am.'

'There's nothing to show,' said Terry, 'that Snitch was killed in the warehouse. He might have been killed elsewhere and brought there afterwards.'

'Why?' Ransom demanded irritably.

'Why was that fellow Swinger killed in a car and put in the boat?' said Terry, and to this the chief inspector had no answer.

'Well,' he said, 'let someone else puzzle it out. We've got our man, and that's all that matters at present.' The telephone on his desk rang. Stretching out his hand, he lifted the receiver. The voice of the night officer in charge came to his ears.

'They've just rung up from Blackheath Police Station, sir,' he reported. 'There's a woman there who says she's the landlady of a lodging-house and she's worried because something's happened to one of her lodgers.'

'Who's her lodger?' grunted Ransom disinterestedly.

'A Miss Catherine Lee,' was the reply, and the chief inspector sat up with a jerk.

25

The Taking of Catherine

Catherine Lee came home a little earlier than usual from Macintyre and Sloan's, and taking off her dripping mackintosh, hung it in the hall and made her way up to her room. She was tired and weary, but she had a lot to think about.

That afternoon she had had her promised interview with Roy Macintyre, and the result had been better than she had expected.

Exchanging her wet shoes for slippers, she sat down in front of the gas fire and warmed her feet while she marshalled her thoughts into something like order.

Nobody knew better than she what a dangerous game she was playing. That moment in the office when Macintyre had surprised her rifling the drawers of his desk had given her a shock she would long remember, and yet her quick brain had been able to turn what might have been disaster into something that was more or less success.

She glanced round the shabby little room and smiled. It would not be long now, she thought, before she would be able to leave this unpleasant environment for an easier and pleasanter life. The thing she had hoped for and schemed for was nearing realization.

It suddenly occurred to her, for no reason at all, to wonder what Jimmy Swann would think if he knew of the understanding between herself and Macintyre. She could picture his horrified face and the look of disillusion in his patient eyes.

She rose at last and crossed over to her little writing-desk. She had two important letters which it was necessary should catch the evening post, and she set to work to get them off her mind. When she had written, sealed and stamped them, she got up with a sigh of relief. It was a beastly night, pouring in torrents, and she decided to spend the rest of the evening with a book.

Her landlady brought her dinner at

eight, offering to post her letters for her, and when she had finished the meal she settled down for a quiet evening. If the room was shabby it was at least cosy, and drawing the curtains to shut out the patter of the rain, she pulled her chair up to the warmth of the gas fire and immersed herself in a novel.

She heard the elderly clerk who occupied the room next to hers come home and softly shut his door, and later the heavy tread of the landlady as she ascended to her bedroom above.

At eleven o'clock she began to feel tired and, laying aside her book, put the kettle on the gas ring to make her usual nightly cup of cocoa. While this was boiling, she slowly undressed, slipped on a dressing-gown, and lit a cigarette.

She made the cocoa carefully, and carrying the cup to her little bedside table, turned out the gas fire and got into bed. By the time she had finished the hot drink, she was feeling thoroughly drowsy, and setting down the empty cup, she switched out the light and snuggled her head into the pillow. In less than five minutes she was asleep . . .

She never knew what it was that woke her or the reason for the fear that accompanied her waking, but suddenly she found herself sitting up in bed, her forehead cold and wet and her heart beating thunderously.

The room was in darkness and she could see nothing; nor, although she listened with straining ears, could she hear anything. And then, out of the silent darkness, a hand closed over her mouth. She almost fainted with terror, but the scream she gave was choked back in her throat.

'Make a sound and you die!' said a harsh, husky voice. 'I want you, Catherine Lee, and if you're sensible you'll come without trouble.'

Her staring eyes, growing accustomed to the darkness, could vaguely make out a dim shape bent over the bed.

'Get up and dress!' went on the voice. 'You can't see the pistol in my hand but you can take my word that it's there, so don't attempt to give the alarm!'

The hand was removed from her mouth, and she felt a cold ring press into her bare shoulder. There was a click, and the light above her bed came on. Blinking fearfully, she saw that the night intruder was an old man with a yellow face and a protruding chin. He was dressed in a shabby black coat and his hands were covered by black gloves.

'Who are you?' she whispered huskily.

'It doesn't matter who I am,' he said. 'Don't raise your voice. Don't make a sound Dress!'

Catherine never forgot the terror of that moment. The sinister figure was like some evil shape conjured up in a nightmare dream. He pulled her dressing-gown off the bed-rail and flung it towards her.

'Get up!' he said again.

With her eyes still fixed on him, she pulled the flimsy garment round her and swung her trembling limbs out of bed. She knew why this man had come, knew for what reason he had taken the risk; and the knowledge turned her blood to water.

As quickly as her shaking hands would let her, she put on her stockings and shoes, slipped a frock on over her night-dress, and hastily tidied her hair.

'Put on your hat and coat!' he ordered, still in the same barely audible whisper.

She obeyed.

'Now open the door, and be careful to make no sound that will wake the house. If you do, it'll be the last sound you ever make.'

She tiptoed into the passage with the other close at her heels; the barrel of the short automatic he held pressed gently into her back as she negotiated the narrow stairs and came into the hall.

'Take off the chain and pull back the bolt,' he said.

She did so, and remembered when last she had stealthily opened that door — the night she had planned her daring excursion to Macintyre's office.

It was still raining heavily as they passed out into the street, and she glanced quickly round, hoping against hope that there might be a strolling policeman in sight. But the dingy street was deserted.

'This way,' said the man at her side, and he turned to the right.

There was one thing she could do, and only one thing. On her little finger she wore a signet ring, and without the old man seeing her she slipped it off and dropped it in the gutter. Her disappearance was bound to become known, and Terry Ward might possibly have a hand in the investigation that would follow. Perhaps he would realize the significance of that ring. It was a wild hope but the only one she had, and with despair in her heart she accompanied her captor to the end of the road.

A closed car with dim lights was waiting drawn up near the kerb, and he motioned her to get in. For an instant it occurred to her to make a dash for it, and then she saw the glint of the weapon in his gloved hand and realized the hopelessness of anything of the sort. She stepped into the interior of the vehicle and he followed, taking his place at the wheel.

The car moved forward, crossed a broad thoroughfare, and turned into a side-street. The man at her side drove with one hand, the other he kept closed round the butt of his pistol.

They negotiated a series of narrow streets, and Catherine guessed that they were making for the river.

'Where are you taking me?' she asked at last, breaking a long silence.

'Wait and see,' answered the old man, and she relapsed again into silence.

Presently, after what seemed an eternity, he brought the car to a halt in a short street lined on either side with high brick walls.

'Get out!' he said curtly. 'We have to go on foot from here.'

She obeyed without protest; in any event, it would be useless and dangerous. She was well aware that the man with her would brook no interference with his plans.

He followed her and took her arm, leading the way through a narrow alley at the end of what she had first taken to be a cul-de-sac. The tang of the river came to her nostrils, and as they came out of the dark passage, she discovered they were standing on a wharf. Tied up to the frontage was a small boat, and he forced her to get into this.

'Take the oars,' he said when he had stepped in beside her. 'You can row.' It was not a question so much as a statement, and she nodded. 'Make for that boat,' he went on as he untied the painter; and following the direction he indicated, she saw a tramp steamer moored in the centre of the stream.

She was wet and shivering with cold as she sent the dinghy towards the boat, but the exercise soon warmed her. She wondered what would happen when they reached their objective, but had little time to speculate as the distance was not a long one. The mooring lights showed blearily through the wet darkness, and presently the boat drifted alongside.

The old man caught a rope ladder that dangled from the deck above and held it taut. 'Up you go,' he said.

She hesitated, eyeing the flimsy structure doubtfully.

'Go on!' he snapped impatiently. 'It's quite safe!'

She began to ascend slowly, and reaching the top, stepped onto the deck of the tramp. A moment later, her companion joined her.

'This way,' he said, and took her

towards the narrow companionway that led below.

She descended into the darkness with the old man close on her heels. Opening a door, he pushed her into an unexpectedly spacious cabin, switching on the light as he did so. Looking around, she gasped with surprise. The outward appearance of the disreputable-looking tramp formed a vivid contrast to the luxury of the inside fittings. The cabin in which she stood was panelled in polished wood, and thick carpets covered the floor. The place was furnished like a millionaire's yacht. He saw her surprise and a chuckle escaped him.

'Not so bad after all, is it?' he remarked. 'Well, you'd better get used to it, for it's going to be your home for a long time to come.'

'What do you intend to do with me?' she inquired calmly, and again he chuckled.

'To a large extent, that will rest with you! If you like to be sensible, no harm will come to you. If not — ' He left the sentence unfinished and shrugged his stooping shoulders. 'I'm afraid,' he went on conversationally, 'that I shall have to take certain precautions before leaving you. I regret having to do so, but in the interests of my safety, it's necessary.' He walked over to an inlaid table, pulled open a drawer, and returned carrying two pairs of handcuffs. 'Hold out your wrists,' he ordered.

It was useless to protest, she realized, and therefore she obeyed calmly. The handcuffs clicked into place.

'Regulation pattern,' he remarked. 'Now sit down.' She sank into a chair, and he clamped the other pair round her ankles. 'Just one more thing,' he murmured, and pocketing the pistol which had never left his hand until now, he took a handkerchief and with a swift movement bound it round her mouth. 'There!' he said when he had finished. 'I'm afraid you'll be a little uncomfortable, but it can't be helped. Now I must go, but I shall be back soon. In the meantime, you'll have to be content to sit in the dark.'

He walked to the door, switched out

the light, and in the darkness that followed she heard it close and the rasp of the key as it turned in the lock.

26

The Ring

The desk sergeant at Blackheath Station looked up as Terry Ward and Chief Inspector Ransom came into the charge-room. Terry's face was white and drawn, for the news which had come over the wire in the early hours of that morning had shaken him.

'This is the woman, sir,' said the grizzled sergeant, indicating a stout, red-faced, dishevelled-looking female who was sitting in a chair in front of the fire. 'We kept her here as you asked. You'd better hear her story.'

The woman's story was brief. Her name was Mrs. Walters and she occupied a house in Union Street. She had gone to bed as usual that night, but had been awakened from a heavy sleep by someone knocking on the front door. Going downstairs to see what the trouble was, she had discovered a policeman who had informed her that the window of her sitting-room was open. Rather alarmed, because she had remembered having closed and latched this early in the evening, she had invited the constable in to make an examination. It was quickly discovered that the latch had been forced. There were scratches round the brass, and on the stained wood surround below several muddy footprints were discovered.

The constable had suggested a search of the house, since it was obvious that someone had broken in, and to this she had eagerly assented. The door of Catherine Lee's bedroom had been found open, and although from the state of the bed she had obviously occupied it, there was no sign of her.

The woman had been puzzled and a little frightened. Her lodger's disappearance, coupled with the open window, suggested all sorts of unpleasant conclusions. She had awakened her husband and also the elderly clerk who occupied the room next to Catherine. The constable had questioned him, but he had heard nothing during the night. It was discovered also that the chain was off the front door and both the bolts drawn back.

'I'm always very careful about locking up the 'ouse,' said Mrs. Walters, 'and I know I shut the window and latched it and bolted and chained the door. What can 'ave 'appened to the young lady?'

Terry said nothing. It was a question he was asking himself — and evading the answer. He looked at Ransom and saw that the chief inspector's face was grave.

'Take us round to your house, Mrs. Walters,' he said; and the landlady, glad of an excuse to get away from the unfamiliar surroundings of the police station, followed them to the waiting police car.

A few minutes later, they drew up outside the house in Union Street. It was a dingy dwelling, exactly like every other house in the street. The door was opened by a small, colourless man with a straggly grey moustache and a bald head, who turned out to be the husband of the woman.

'It's a funny thing,' declared Mr. Walters. 'I can't understand it. Do you think it's possible the young lady can have gone off with someone?'

Terry thought it very possible, but not exactly in the way Mr. Walters was suggesting.

They made an examination of the sitting-room and discovered everything as the constable had reported. There was no doubt that somebody had skilfully forced back the catch and effected an entrance by the window. The wet footprints had dried, but their muddy outline was still visible and could be traced across the square of carpet to the door. Outside in the hall there was no further sign of them, neither could they discover any traces on the stairway.

An examination of the woman's bed-room brought to light the fact that her night-dress was missing. There were several others in a chest of drawers but none of these had been worn, and they were forced to come to the conclusion that at the time she had left the house she had been wearing the night-dress. A pair of shoes, a skirt, a jacket and a coat were also missing.

'It doesn't look too good to me,' said Chief Inspector Ransom, when they had completed their examination. 'It's fairly easy to see what happened. Somebody broke into the house and forced this woman to dress and accompany them. The question is — who?'

It was a question that was worrying Terry. Who could have been responsible for the disappearance of Catherine? Certainly not Macintyre, who was at that moment safely confined in a cell at Cannon Row Station, unless he had given the order for her abduction before his arrest. This was possible, and on reflection seemed the only conceivable theory. Catherine, during her work at Macintyre and Sloan's, had discovered something that was dangerous to Macintyre's safety, and he had arranged to put her somewhere where she couldn't talk.

He mentioned this theory to Ransom. The chief inspector grunted.

'Maybe,' he said. 'The thing is to find Catherine and find her as soon as possible.'

With this Terry heartily agreed. 'Let's

see if there's anything to be found outside,' he suggested, and leaving the disordered bedroom, they made their way down the stairs to the front door.

It had ceased raining, and the clear light of dawn showed up the street in all its drab ugliness. In spite of the fact that the people in this district were early risers, there was no sign or sight of a soul. The police driver sat stolidly at the wheel of his car and took no notice of either Terry or the chief inspector as they surveyed the outside of the house.

'These places, with the door opening straight on to the pavement, are the answer to the burglar's prayer,' said Ransom. 'Our man merely had to walk down the street, make sure there was nobody looking, stop opposite the window, and force back the catch at his leisure. Luckily in this type of house, there's usually very little to attract the ordinary type of burglar.'

'Well, there's nothing much to see here. We'd better get back to the Yard and send out a description of Catherine to all stations. That's the first and most obvious thing to do. Maybe somebody will come forward who saw her.'

He moved over to the waiting police car and Terry followed him. It was just as he was stepping into the machine that he made his discovery. Something bright caught his eye, and stooping, he picked from the gutter a ring. His heart leapt as he saw it and he turned to Ransom.

'This is Catherine's ring,' he said, and was unconscious of the fact that he had used her Christian name. 'I remember noticing it on her little finger when I first went up to interview Macintyre.'

The chief inspector took the signet ring from him and examined it, frowning. 'How did it get in the gutter?' he muttered. 'Was it pulled off in a struggle, or did she deliberately drop it there?'

Terry examined the vicinity of his find. 'There's no sign of a struggle,' he said. 'More likely she dropped it in the hope that it would provide us with a clue.'

'Hm!' said Ransom, twisting the ring about between his finger and thumb. 'Well, it doesn't help us much, merely shows what we knew before, that she passed this way last night. Keep this for the time being, Ward, maybe it will prove useful later on, but I can't see that it's of much value at the moment.'

Terry slipped the ring into his waistcoat pocket. Neither could he — then; though the ring was to prove of inestimable value later, and bring about the downfall of the unknown controller of the River Men.

They got into the police car and were rapidly driven to Scotland Yard. Ransom scribbled a message that was sent to the information room and from there relayed to every police station in the country. The printing press in the Yard's private newspaper department began to work at full speed, and two hours later, messengers on bicycles and in motorcars began distributing sheets wet from the press to patrolling policemen in outlying districts containing a complete description of the missing woman, and asking for any information concerning her whereabouts.

'D'you know this man Copping who Macintyre mentioned?' asked Ransom when these preliminaries had been completed.

'Yes, he's quite a well-known figure on the riverside,' Terry answered. 'He's a pal of Joe Hickman's, the fellow who runs that billiard saloon at Woolwich.'

'I think we'd better pull him in. According to Macintyre's story, we've got evidence to charge him under the Dangerous Drug Act, and there's a chance that he may know something about tonight's business. I'll leave that to you, Ward.'

'O.K., sir,' said Terry, and he left the Yard. A police car carried him to Wapping headquarters, and during the journey he puzzled his brain to think of something that would put him on the track of Catherine. He was intensely worried about her. A voice within him whispered that she was in danger. If only she could have left something behind more tangible than the ring.

He took the little gold circlet from his pocket and looked at it. What a pity that she could not have left some message instead of that, something that would have told them who was responsible for spiriting her away and where she had been taken. Of course she had not had time to write anything. The man who had come for her would see to that. The dropping of the ring was the only thing she could do, and she had probably done it as a forlorn hope. And yet the discovery of it where it had been found meant nothing. It didn't even supply the direction in which she had gone. She might have gone up the street or down the street. The ring had been found exactly outside the front door.

Terry remembered it well. She had worn it on the little ringer of her right hand, and it was almost the first thing he had noticed when he had met her. It was obviously not a woman's ring. It was too big and heavy; probably it had been left her by a near relation, maybe her father or her uncle, or perhaps a brother. Women seldom, as a rule, wore a signet ring unless there was some sort of sentimental value attached to it.

He was replacing the pathetic little souvenir in his pocket when a wild idea occurred to him. It couldn't be possible! And yet, if this startling thought which occurred to him was true, then Catherine's action in leaving behind the ring had been prompted by a very real purpose. Had that been her intention? Had she left the ring on the chance that its significance would appeal to someone? That it would be found by a person who would be clever enough to understand what it meant?

Terry believed that he had found the right answer; and if he had, then things were not as hopeless as they seemed, for if he had read Catherine's reason for leaving behind the ring aright, then he was in the position to lay his hands on the man at the head of the river thieves just whenever he pleased.

27

Mr. Copping Spills the Beans

Joe Hickman, a cigar between his lips, picked up the wad of notes which the olive-skinned little man before him had just handed to him and rapidly counted them.

'There's a fiver short! Come on, Stiney, don't try them tricks on me!'

'It was all right when I give it yer, Hickman!' protested Mr. Stienman. 'You saw me count it!'

'Come on!' said Joe Hickman threateningly. 'Hand over that fiver, you miserable little rat, or I'll skin you alive!'

The little man sighed and allowed the note which he had skilfully palmed to flutter to the desk. 'My 'and was 'ot and it must 'ave stuck to it,' he said. 'Sorry, Joe.'

'You'd 'ave been sorrier if you 'adn't parted,' said Mr. Hickman. 'Well, that completes the deal, Stiney. The place is yours. A pretty good bargain you've got.'

'I don't know about that,' muttered Mr. Stienman. 'You made the price pretty heavy, Hickman.'

Joe Hickman stowed the thick wad of notes away in his pocket. 'It was up to you,' he remarked. 'I told you what I wanted and you paid it. You needn't have paid it if you didn't want to.'

It had not been quite as easy as this; for over a week they had wrangled and argued concerning the purchase price of Mr. Hickman's billiard saloon, and that gentleman had stuck out for the last farthing.

'The property becomes yours from tomorrow,' he said complacently, 'and I shan't be sorry to see the last of it. Not that I 'aven't made a pretty good thing out of it. I've done very well, Stiney, and if you runs it on the same lines as I have you'll do very well, too.' He looked up as the door of his office opened and Copping came in. 'Hello, Steve!' he greeted cheerfully. 'Well, I've sold the old 'ome lock, stock and barrel. Stiney 'ere's the new proprietor.'

Copping did not appear interested in either Mr. Stienman or his friend's news. 'They took Macintyre last night!' he said abruptly.

'Took him last night?' echoed Hickman. 'Where?'

'There was a raid on Gallows Wharf. Give us a drink, Joe.'

Hickman reached towards his cupboard and produced a bottle of whisky and glasses. 'A raid?' he asked inquiringly.

'Yes, the place was surrounded from the land side and the river, and when Macintyre got there they closed in and took him.'

Mr. Hickman whistled slowly. 'So that's why the big fellow instructed you to arrange to meet Macintyre at the place,' he muttered.

'That's why,' said Copping, and he swallowed the neat whisky which the other had poured out. 'And they found the dead body of Snitch Keller, too.'

Hickman's eyes opened wide. 'Keller?' he growled. 'What had he got to do with it?'

'I don't know. But they found him all

the same. His 'ead 'ad been bashed in and he was dead as a pole-axed ox.'

'Well, I can't say I'm sorry. I never did like that feller. I always had my suspicions about him, Steve. Always thought he was a copper's nark.'

'I never liked him either. The question is, Joe, what do we do now?'

'Clear!' said Hickman briefly. 'I'm going today. If you're wise, you'll come with me.'

Steve Copping wiped his damp face. 'I'm wise,' he said. 'Ever since I heard about last night's business, I've been scared stiff. If that feller Macintyre tells the busies *who* arranged to meet him at Gallows Wharf, they'll be on me like flies.'

'Well, don't stop 'ere, then,' said Mr. Hickman in alarm. 'If you think there's a likelihood of the busies being after you, you'd better clear out as soon as possible. I don't want any trouble here, there's nothing at present to connect me with anything, and — '

The buzzer in the corner of his room rang softly and his big face went grey. 'They're here now,' he said, and he swung round angrily towards Copping. 'It's your fault,' he snarled. 'You've led the busies here. If you thought there was a chance of them cottoning on to you, why didn't you keep clear? By God, I'd like to wring — '

He half rose to his feet, and Mr. Stienman put out a trembling and protesting hand.

'Steady, Hickman,' he warned. 'If the busies are here, you don't want to make more trouble. Anyway, I'm going. I'm not in it.'

He got up swiftly, and at that moment the door was flung open and Terry Ward, with half a dozen men at his heels, filled the entrance. His stern eyes glanced round the tiny smoke-laden office quickly.

'I want you, Copping,' he said. 'Hello, Stienman, what are you doing in this outfit?'

'I'm not doing anything, Mr. Ward,' whined Stiney. 'I've just bought the property from Mr. Hickman, that's why I'm here. Just concluding an honest piece of business, that's all.'

'So you've bought the property, have you?' said Terry slowly. 'Getting cold feet, Hickman?'

'A man's entitled to sell his business, isn't he?' snarled Joe. 'Is there any law against that?'

'No, you can sell as many businesses as you like,' Terry replied. 'But you'll sell 'em for the next seven years from Dartmoor.'

'What d'you mean?' asked the big man, his face the colour of putty. 'You're not pullin' me in?'

'I'm pulling you and your friend Copping in!' snapped Terry. 'I want you under a charge of smuggling dangerous drugs into the country!'

'I don't know what you mean, Mr. Ward,' said Steve Copping, his face the picture of injured innocence. 'You don't think I'd do a thing like that, do you? It's a dirty game. I'd rather cut off me right 'and!'

'It's no good, Copping,' interrupted Terry. 'Macintyre's squealed. Maybe if you tell us what we want to know, you'll be let off lightly. Now, I'm not wasting any further time. Come on!'

There was nothing against Mr. Stienman and he was allowed to go, but Hickman and Copping were escorted to the waiting police car and driven to Scotland Yard.

Here Chief Inspector Ransom was waiting to receive them, and they were closely questioned.

'I don't know who the feller is,' said Copping after his resistance had been beaten down and he had told all he knew concerning the River Men. 'He used to phone up Hickman and give me my instructions. Sometimes I'd meet him at Gallows Wharf and he'd give me detailed typewritten plans for a coup. But who he is or what he is I don't know. He's an old feller with a queer, yellowish sort of face and a protrudin' chin.'

'It wasn't Macintyre?' snapped Ransom.

''*Im*! No, it weren't him. This old feller was anxious to get him involved, I don't know why. He made me put up the proposition to Macintyre about the drugs, and he also made me write to him and arrange to meet him at Gallows Wharf last night.'

'What do you know about that box that was delivered to the Chatterton Hotel?' said the chief inspector abruptly.

'I don' know nothin' about that,' muttered Copping, but his face belied his words.

'Come across, Copping. If you come clean, we may be able to help you.'

'I didn't know there was anythin' wrong about it. S'elp me Gawd, I didn't! Macintyre asked me to find someone to take it to the district messenger office and have it delivered. He said it was nothin', only some drugs that some friends of his from America wanted and found difficulty in getting.'

'Why did the woman you arranged with say her name was Catherine Lee?' demanded Terry.

'That was the old man's idea,' answered Copping. 'Everything that passed between me and Macintyre I reported to him; those were his instructions. When he 'eard about this box, he told me to get 'old of a woman to take it to the district messenger office and say that her name was Catherine Lee. I found a woman, but she didn't carry out my orders to the letter. She thought there was something fishy about the thing and was afraid to go to the office herself, so she got hold of a feller she found in Villiers Street and — '

'We know the rest,' broke in Ransom.

'So you've no idea who this old man is?'

Steve Copping shook his head violently. 'No, I ain't! And that's the truth!'

'All right,' said Ransom, 'we'll see you later.'

Mr. Copping was taken away and Joe Hickman sent for, but he could offer no more information than his friend. He received messages from the unknown which he relayed to Copping, but he had no idea of his identity.

'And we're going to have difficulty in finding him,' said the chief inspector to Terry when Mr. Hickman had been escorted to the cells. 'He's very cleverly hedged himself in.'

Terry said nothing; he believed that he had found the old man who controlled the River Men, but his theory was so wild and improbable that he thought it best to keep it to himself until he could offer proof.

28

Downriver

To Catherine Lee, a prisoner in the luxurious cabin of the tramp, time seemed to pass on leaden feet. It was quite dark, the portholes of the cabin had been blocked up and she had no idea, beyond a vague guess, as to the hour. She heard the river gradually wake to life, the hooting of tugs and the thousand and one noises that denoted a fresh day's work was starting.

Occasionally the moored boat rocked in the wash of some heavy ship as it passed, but nobody came near her and she heard no signs of life on board.

The terror of that moment of awakening when she had discovered the sinister figure of the old man at her bedside had passed. Although her peril was still as acute, she no longer felt the intense and numbing fear which had gripped her

305

then. She knew that it could not be long before her absence was discovered and the police were notified, and she prayed that the ring she had left had fallen into the hands of someone with sufficient intelligence to understand its meaning. There was a ray of hope in this; faint, but still something to catch hold of. That every effort would be made to trace her she was sure, and this knowledge helped to bolster her courage.

The hours dragged wearily by, and she began to feel hungry; but it was unlikely, she concluded, that her captor would return until nightfall. She would have to possess herself in patience. Presently she fell into a fitful sleep; her disturbed rest of the night, and the shock she had experienced, had left her tired.

She had no idea what time it was when she woke, but there were movements above her head and the sound of footsteps on the deck. She heard the rumble of something being taken aboard. There were a number of footsteps, and she thought at first that perhaps the police had tracked her down; but after listening for a little while, she concluded that they were made by the crew.

She tried desperately to work the gag away from her mouth, but although she moved her jaws until they ached, it had been too well tied. It was useless to attempt to free her hands or ankles; she might have been able to deal with cords, but the steel handcuffs were beyond her.

The rumbling continued, and presently it occurred to her what it was. The tramp was coaling! They were preparing for a journey. Her heart sank as she realized the significance of this. If they were going downriver to the open sea, it was unlikely that the police would find her in time. It was stupid she had not realized this possibility before, but it had never occurred to her. And yet it was the logical outcome of her being brought on board. She had concluded at first that it had been because the tramp provided a more suitable hiding place than anywhere else, one less likely to be discovered. But she ought to have reasoned that it was more likely because it offered a better getaway for the man who held her.

She was thankful for one thing. The noise and bustle above her helped to distract her thoughts and make the time pass less slowly.

Somebody came down and tried the cabin door, and she heard a guttural voice shout: 'Leave that alone, can't yer! You're not supposed to go in there. Anyway, it's locked.'

The person who had tried the door muttered an apology, and she heard the sound of his retreating footsteps.

A long interval passed, and then she heard the hiss of steam. The furnaces had been lighted, and the ship was evidently being prepared for departure. The boat shuddered and began to vibrate as the engine started. There was a rattle of chains and winches, and she heard the muffled tone of a man's voice shouting orders, and then the thrash of a propeller.

The vessel began to move slowly; they were on their way!

The realization that she was leaving all possible chance of salvation brought Catherine to the verge of despair. There was something final about that steady movement that made her panic-stricken, and she was powerless to do anything but submit. She could hear the wash of water above the throb-throb of the pulsating engine.

The forward motion was scarcely perceptible now, and only by the quivering of the whole structure was she aware that the boat was still moving.

Her thoughts flew to Terry Ward. It was likely that she would never see him again. Once this boat reached the open sea, it would be easy to arrange her transference to a larger vessel, and so she would pass beyond the ken of man . . .

In spite of her self-control, she felt the hot tears flood to her eyes until they smarted, but by a supreme effort she kept them back. It was useless crying; perhaps even now something might occur to rescue her from this horrible position.

The sound of feet descending a ladder near the door of the cabin interrupted her thoughts. A second later, she heard a key grate in the lock and the door was opened, emitting a dim flood of light. Silhouetted against this she could see the figure of the old man.

He came in, raised his hand and pressed the switch. The lights flashed on, and closing the door, he locked it behind him.

'Well,' he said, 'I daresay the time has passed slowly. I'm sorry but I could find no means to make your waiting more pleasurable for you. I've no doubt you're hungry, and in a few hours I shall be able to provide you with a meal. At present it is impossible. You no doubt realize that we are moving downriver. Until we reach the open sea, I have no wish to take the captain and crew of this boat into my confidence concerning you. At the present moment, they are not aware of your presence; that I shall break to them later. In case you imagine that they may be prepared to assist you, I can assure you they will not. They are all foreigners, and with the exception of the captain, completely ignorant of the English tongue. The captain is an Italian and so are most of the crew. The few who are not are Dutch. You're starting a new life, Catherine. It depends on you whether you make it a happy one or whether you prefer it to be short and miserable.'

His voice changed. 'Since I first saw you, I realized you were the only woman in the world for me, and I was determined that when the end came, I would take you with me. I don't think there's any need for me to tell you this; I think you've realized it all along, as you've realized a great number of other things. It was only recently that I discovered who you were and why you'd sought employment at Macintyre and Sloan's, but the knowledge did nothing to change my regard for you.

'On board this boat is more money than you can realize; money that's mine and which, if you're sensible, can become yours. Lying out to sea, off the Nore Light, is a yacht awaiting us. On board that yacht, we can be married and sail to a life of ease and luxury in a warmer and pleasanter country than this fog-bound, rainy England; a country of sunshine and colour, of joy and life, of happiness and love. It needs but a word from you, and you'll be free to board that yacht, not as a prisoner but as its mistress.'

He must have seen the horror and loathing in her eyes, for his voice changed. 'You're a fool!' he said harshly. 'It makes no difference to my plans whether you agree or not. If you refuse to come willingly, I shall take you by force. Everything I've planned and schemed for I have achieved, and I need you to make my victory complete. If you're under any delusion that Terry Ward will help you, you can put it out of your mind now. He's dead!'

She flinched, and the sight evidently gave him satisfaction, for he chuckled. 'That hurt you,' he said. 'I've known for a long time that you were getting sentimental over that policeman. Well, you'll never see him again; he's lying at the bottom of the Thames with a hundredweight of chain around him — food for the fishes!'

There was something in his eyes that told her he was lying; that this story was a fabrication intended to break her spirit.

'I'm leaving you now,' he said abruptly. 'Next time I come, I'll bring you some food.'

He was in the act of turning away when she felt the vessel jar from stem to stem as the engines were suddenly reversed. The man with her uttered an exclamation and hastily unlocked the door. Locking it behind him, his footsteps hurried up the ladder, followed by an excited altercation.

The boat had ceased moving, and Catherine's heart leaped as it occurred to her what this might signify. Was it possible that at the last moment help had arrived?

She heard a scraping, bumping sound near at hand, and guessed that it was a boat that had come alongside the vessel. A shot rang out, followed by another and another, and a muffled scream of pain reached her ears and a confused tramping of feet overhead.

She heard a sharp, authoritative voice barking a succession of orders, there came another fusillade of shots, and then the sound of stumbling feet in the passageway outside the cabin in which she was confined. The lock clicked back, the door was flung open, and her captor stumbled across the threshold, slamming it to behind him.

She saw the pistol in his hand and the expression on his face, and but for the gag would have screamed. He came over to her side, and crouching, faced the door. Even as he did so, there came a thudding on the panel.

'Open this door! Open in the king's name!' cried a voice; and Catherine could have swooned with delight, for it was the voice of Terry Ward!

29

The Capture

The man at her side gripped her arm, and she felt the barrel of the pistol pressed against her neck.

'Tell him if he attempts to break open the door that I shall kill you,' he said, and taking his hand from her arm, tore the gag from her lips.

'Open this door!' cried Terry's voice again. 'Open this door or we'll break it in!'

'He's threatened to shoot me if you do that!' cried Catherine, and although her voice was husky from disuse and the dryness of her throat, it reached him.

'Is that you, Catherine?' he called. 'Are you all right?'

'I'm all right at present,' she answered. 'But be careful, Terry; he's covering me with a gun.'

There was silence, followed by a mutter

of voices as Terry passed on the news to the men with him.

'What's the good of threatening Miss Lee?' asked the young inspector after a pause. 'You can't get away. We know who you are. You might just as well give in.'

'Come and get me!' snarled Jimmy Swann, and he tore off the thin painted rubber mask which had formed his disguise. 'Come and get me, Ward. Before you can put your foot across the threshold, Catherine will die!'

There was a tinge of foam round his lips, and his eyes glared hard. Catherine, catching sight of his face, shuddered. Was this the gentle Jimmy S she had known? Was this the man whose many kindnesses she had so appreciated? Whose genial personality had been beloved by the staff at Macintyre and Sloan's? This snarling thing with foam-flecked mouth and distorted face? She knew it was. Had known that Jimmy Swann was responsible for her abduction ever since he had appeared at her bedside, for beneath the harsh voice he adopted in his disguise as the old man, she had recognized his own.

There was no sound outside the door, and she wondered what Terry was doing. It was a difficult situation. There was no means of reaching Swann except by breaking down the communicating door, and at the first sign of attack on that, he would shoot her. She knew that his threat was no bluff; could see it in the glitter of his eyes. The last-minute failure of his plans had turned him into a raving maniac. The brilliant brain which had conceived and controlled the River Men had broken down under the strain.

'Get me, will they?' he chuckled. 'We'll go together, Catherine, you and I together, as we planned!'

She shivered and he looked at her, his expression softening. 'You needn't be afraid,' he whispered. 'I'll be with you. Death is not so very terrible. I've seen many men die: the detective they sent to trap me, that stupid fool of a clerk who found out that I was leading a double life and thought he would blackmail me, the man who would have betrayed me to Terry Ward and his scum! I saw them all die, and it was very easy. There's nothing in death, just a quiet, dreamless sleep.'

She made no answer. She was racking her brains to come up with a solution to the impossible situation, but she could think of nothing.

The circular ring of the automatic coldly touched her neck and warned her of her danger. Outside the door, all was quiet and still. There was no sound from Terry, and Catherine wondered what he was planning. She failed to see what he could do.

'I've beaten them,' chuckled the man at her side. 'Old Jimmy S has proved too clever for them once again! They thought they'd got me, but they haven't. I've got the whip hand and they can't do anything.'

'You always were very clever, Jimmy,' she said pleasantly, and although her heart was beating rapidly, her voice was cool and calm. 'I always admired you.'

'Did you?' he said. 'D'you think I'm clever, Catherine? I'm glad to hear you say that. Why didn't you tell me so before and save me all this trouble?'

'You knew I always thought so,' she answered.

'I hoped you did,' he replied. 'D'you remember when you first came to the office, how I used to put flowers in the vase on your desk and give you the little cakes you liked for tea?'

'You were always very kind,' she murmured.

'I fell in love with you the first time I saw you. Did you know that? I thought you were the most wonderful thing in the world. I still think there's nothing half so lovely.'

He had removed the pistol and was bending over her. Was Terry listening? she wondered desperately. Would he understand?

'Can't you get rid of those policemen?' she murmured. 'We don't want them, do we, Jimmy?'

'No, no,' he said quickly. 'But what can I do?'

'I'll help you if you'll take these things off my hands.'

'I can't do that.' There was suspicion in his voice and her heart sank. 'You're fond of Ward; you'd help him trap me.'

'Undo my hands, Jimmy,' she said

softly, and he hesitated; and then to her relief, he put the pistol down on the floor and began to feel in his pockets.

'What did I do with the key?' he muttered. 'Ah, I know. Here it is.' He pulled it out and unlocked the handcuffs at her wrists.

With a quick movement she tore her hands free, and stooping, snatched up the pistol from the floor.

'It's all right, Terry!' she cried. 'Break in the door. I've got the pistol!'

'Right!' sang out Terry's voice, and almost before the word had left his lips, there was a shattering crash and the polished door shivered.

Swann uttered a snarl of rage. 'I'll kill you for that!' he hissed, and sprang at her.

Her finger tightened on the trigger, and the noise of the report was deafening in that confined space; but the bullet went wide, burying itself in the panelled wall. The next moment, he was on her and had borne her backwards. The pistol flew from her hands as his fingers closed round her throat.

'Terry!' she shrieked.

With a splintering crash, the cabin door collapsed and Terry, followed by two burly river policemen, sprang across the threshold. They tore Swann away from Catherine only just in time. Her face was blue already from the strangling fingers which had nearly cut short her life.

30

The Finish

James Swann, a gibbering, obscene thing, was taken by launch to Wapping Headquarters and from thence to Scotland Yard, The surprise of Chief Inspector Ransom was almost ludicrous when Terry handed over his prisoner.

'Swann?' he exclaimed. 'That's the fellow who was general manager of Macintyre and Sloan's, isn't it?'

'That's the fellow,' said Terry. 'And who was also instigator and controller of the River Men.'

'Well, it's a smart piece of work, Ward,' said the chief inspector. 'How did you get on to him?'

Terry explained.

'It was really Miss Lee who put me on to him,' he said. 'You remember that ring she left in the gutter on the night he took her from her lodgings?'

Ransom nodded.

'Well, it occurred to me,' went on Terry, 'that there must be some reason for her leaving it there apart from just letting us know that she had passed that way. Thinking the matter over, I came to the conclusion that it was a very subtle reason. If you come to think of it, sir, there were only two people who could have been interested in getting Miss Lee out of the way: Macintyre, or somebody connected with the firm of Macintyre and Sloan. Obviously, since she'd been in their employ for three years, it must have been someone connected with that firm who would have had any interest in her removal. It couldn't have been Macintyre, unless he had arranged for it to be done before his arrest, which I was rather doubtful of. And then I remembered that the general manager's name was Swann. Almost immediately, the significance of the ring occurred to me. It was Miss Lee's effort to tell the police or whoever found it the name of her abductor.'

'I still don't see,' Ransom remarked. 'How could the ring do that?'

'It was a *signet* ring,' said Terry. 'Do you see now?'

Ransom's eyes opened. 'By Jove!' he said. 'Of course. The connection between cygnet and swan!'

'Right!' said Terry. 'The one automatically suggests the other.'

'I doubt if it would ever have occurred to me in a thousand years,' declared Ransom candidly. 'Of course, when you point it out, it's obvious.'

'I think Miss Lee hoped that I should hear about it. Isn't that right?' asked Terry.

'Yes,' she answered. 'You see, it was the only thing I could do. I knew Terry — Mr. Ward — ' The chief inspector gave no sign that he had noticed the slip. ' — knew Swann, and I hoped he'd see the connection.'

'You've been watching him for a long time, Miss Lee, haven't you?' said Ransom. Again she nodded. 'For three years. They told me that at the public prosecutor's office,' said the chief inspector, 'when they telephoned over immediately on hearing that you were missing.'

Terry looked at him in amazement.

'The public prosecutor's office?' he gasped.

Ransom's grey eyes twinkled. 'You didn't know that? Yes, Miss Lee is one of us. She's a detective employed by the public prosecutor's department, and during the lifetime of old Macintyre, she was sent down to join the firm at his request to inquire into some irregularities concerning certain goods which had mysteriously disappeared from the warehouse. Old Macintyre suspected Swann, but he could discover no proof. And neither could Miss Lee. She was on the point of giving it up when the River Men became active; and the prosecutor's office, who were under the impression that the reason why the activities of these river thieves could not be checked was because there was someone in the police force working with them, decided to let her stay on in the hope that she could discover something. She didn't, but she got on the track of Macintyre and his drug campaign. Although for a long time she had been suspicious of Swann, she couldn't find any proof.'

'So that accounts for the attack that was made on you some nights ago,' said Terry.

'That accounts for it,' answered Catherine brightly. 'I received an anonymous letter advising me that if I wanted to discover who was at the bottom of the River Men, to go to Balkans Wharf. It was a trap, of course, and I half suspected it was, but I went all the same. You know the result,' she added ruefully.

'Well, anyway, we've caught the fellow,' remarked Ransom. 'And we've caught Macintyre as well; though, by the way, his name isn't Macintyre and never was. The report's come over from America concerning the Renfrews, and this fellow Macintyre is a man called Micky Dean who used to run with a gang in New York of which the Renfrews were members. The real Macintyre was a dope. He died at Micky Dean's lodgings; and Micky, who was in some difficulty himself, pinched his identity. When old Macintyre died and Roy Macintyre was being advertised for, Micky Dean saw an opportunity of getting into money quickly. He established his identity and came over to England as Roy Hugh Macintyre, the man who had been buried in the name of Micky Dean in America.'

'And I suppose the Renfrews followed him to get their cut?' said Terry.

Ransom nodded. 'That's it. And they got the wrong cut! This fellow Dean is a dangerous man, but nothing is more certain than that he'll hang.'

'And Swann?' said Terry.

The chief inspector pursed his lips. 'I doubt if he'll ever be executed,' he said, shaking his head. 'He's as crazy as a coot, and unless I'm very much mistaken, he'll end up at Broadmoor.'

He was right. At the end of the long trial, which followed in due course, the jury, without retiring, brought in a verdict of 'Guilty but insane' against James Swann, and he was sentenced to life imprisonment in the big building among the Berkshire Hills which houses those unfortunates who are criminally insane.

On the evening of the sentence, Terry Ward met Catherine for dinner. She was a very different woman to the one he had known at Greenwich: radiant and smartly dressed; and he looked at her a little shyly.

'You know,' he said halfway through the meal, 'I wish you'd really been a secretary.'

She looked at him in surprise. 'Why?'

'It would have made things much easier in many ways.'

'Tell me one of them,' she begged.

'Well, an inspector's pay in the river police isn't exactly equal to a Rothschild's income.'

'Neither is the salary of a member of the public prosecutor's department!' she retorted.

He eyed her expensive frock, and she laughed.

'This was a present,' she remarked. 'I think Sir Richard — ' She referred to the public prosecutor. ' — wanted to make up for my long sojourn in a combined room in Union Street.' She gave a little shiver. 'If you knew how thankful I am to see the last of it . . . '

Terry crumbled his roll and surveyed the cruet tentatively. 'My idea of an ideal residence,' he said, 'is a small cottage on the banks of the river, somewhere in the upper reaches, with a garden, a little car and — '

'And what?' she asked softly.

He told her, and she decided that even on the modest salary of an inspector in the river police, it was possible for all his ambitions to be realized.

THE FACELESS ONES
GRIM DEATH
MURDER IN MANUSCRIPT
THE GLASS ARROW
THE THIRD KEY
THE ROYAL FLUSH MURDERS
THE SQUEALER
MR. WHIPPLE EXPLAINS
THE SEVEN CLUES
THE CHAINED MAN
THE HOUSE OF THE GOAT
THE FOOTBALL POOL MURDERS
THE HAND OF FEAR
SORCERER'S HOUSE
THE HANGMAN
THE CON MAN
MISTER BIG
THE JOCKEY
THE SILVER HORSESHOE
THE TUDOR GARDEN MYSTERY
THE SHOW MUST GO ON
SINISTER HOUSE
THE WITCHES' MOON
ALIAS THE GHOST
THE LADY OF DOOM

THE BLACK HUNCHBACK
PHANTOM HOLLOW
WHITE WIG
THE GHOST SQUAD
THE NEXT TO DIE
THE WHISPERING WOMAN
THE TWELVE APOSTLES
THE GRIM JOKER
THE HUNTSMAN
THE NIGHTMARE MURDERS
THE TIPSTER
THE VAMPIRE MAN
THE RED TAPE MURDERS
THE FRIGHTENED MAN
THE TOKEN
MR. MIDNIGHT

With Chris Verner:
THE BIG FELLOW
THE SNARK WAS A BOOJUM
THE SEVENTH VIRGIN

We do hope that you have enjoyed reading this large print book.

Did you know that all of our titles are available for purchase?

We publish a wide range of high quality large print books including:

Romances, Mysteries, Classics
General Fiction
Non Fiction and Westerns

Special interest titles available in large print are:

The Little Oxford Dictionary
Music Book, Song Book
Hymn Book, Service Book

Also available from us courtesy of Oxford University Press:

Young Readers' Dictionary
(large print edition)
Young Readers' Thesaurus
(large print edition)

For further information or a free brochure, please contact us at:

Ulverscroft Large Print Books Ltd.,
The Green, Bradgate Road, Anstey,
Leicester, LE7 7FU, England.
Tel: (00 44) **0116 236 4325**
Fax: (00 44) **0116 234 0205**

THE MISSING MAN

V. J. Banis

Writer Cindy Carter accepts a routine assignment from her editor: fly to Athens, write some articles, and fit in an interview with an elderly professor who insists he's got something important to say. But what occurs is anything but routine. Her case is accidentally switched with that of another passenger containing one hundred thousand dollars in cash. When the professor is killed in an explosion, Cindy becomes embroiled in an assassination plot involving a Russian terrorist, and must assist NATO agents in capturing the missing man.

BETTY BLAKE

N. M. Scott

Featuring an amazingly perceptive Edwardian child blessed with a talent for solving village puzzles, Betty Blake provides us with a glimpse of a future amateur detective in the making. Betty begins her sleuthing at age nine continuing through to age twelve. Her cases include pillar box puzzles to headless ducks, a stolen emerald ring and the death of a solicitor's wife — not to mention a ghostly disturbance on a golf course. For someone so young and precocious — no case is a burden or unsolvable!

THE TREASURE HUNTERS

Norman Firth

Gilda Baxter decides to call unannounced at her fiancé's cottage on a surprise visit . . . only to learn on her arrival that his boat, badly damaged, had been found floating overturned in the bay, and that he is missing — presumed drowned . . . Diana Russell is on a mission to help her twin sister stop a man from blackmailing and ruining her life. For her plan to succeed, she must put herself in great danger — but sometimes best laid plans have a habit of going awry . . .

SHERLOCK HOLMES: THE FOUR-HANDED GAME

Paul D. Gilbert

Holmes and Watson find themselves bombarded with an avalanche of dramatic cases! Holmes enrols Inspectors Lestrade and Bradstreet to help him play a dangerous four-handed game against an organization whose power and influence seems to know no bounds. As dissimilar as the cases seem to be — robbery, assault, and gruesome murder — Holmes suspects that each one has been meticulously designed to lure him towards a conclusion that even he could not have anticipated. However, when his brother Mycroft goes missing, he realises that he is running out of time . . .